Love Renewed in Oakbrook City

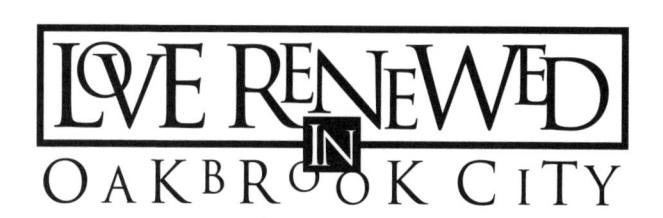

Kathryn Jameson

WINEPRESS WP PUBLISHING

© 1998 by Kathryn Jameson. All rights reserved

Printed in the United States of America

Packaged by WinePress Publishing, PO Box 1406, Mukilteo, WA 98275. The views expressed or implied in this work do not necessarily reflect those of WinePress Publishing. Ultimate design, content, and editorial accuracy of this work is the responsibility of the author(s).

No part of this publication may be reproduced, stored in a retrieval system, or transmitted in any way by any means—electronic, mechanical, photocopy, recording, or otherwise—without the prior permission of the copyright holder, except as provided by USA copyright law.

ISBN 1-57921-149-6
Library of Congress Catalog Card Number: 98-61306

INTRODUCTION

This story is about one Christian woman's growing awareness of what is truly going on around her. What Saralyn Green slowly becomes aware of is that all things are not as they appear. She goes to church on Sunday, belongs to a Bible-study group, and loves her family dearly. Her family and friends live in, what most believe to be, a safe, crime-free neighborhood north of Los Angeles.

For years, Saralyn had kept any real threat of romance at a distance. Now there are two men in her life: Daniel, her friend; and Matthew, the new employee at the recycling center, which Saralyn owns and manages with the help of her foreman, Benjamin.

After working for many years in the corporate world, Saralyn has paid her dues. She now runs her own business, loves her two daughters, and has wonderful friends. But what strange things are happening around Oakbrook City? Who is the true enemy?

Part One

Summer 1999

Chapter One

It was a beautiful, sunny day. No one on earth could have predicted the bizarre series of events that were about to unfold during the next several months.

Saralyn was grateful for the good weather as she turned on the office computer system. The small clock on the computer screen told her the time: 8:30 A.M. *I am lucky, after all these years, to finally have a job that I really enjoy waking up for,* she mused.

When Saralyn first arrived that morning, she had seen the men working outside her large office windows. For the majority of them, the day had started an hour ago. Most of the company's crew usually left no later than three-thirty or four o'clock in the afternoon, unless a large, late shipment of materials was due to arrive. She, however, often remained several hours after everyone else had left for the day.

After working in the corporate environment for more than fifteen years, Saralyn had started a recycling business three years ago. Now she was the boss. The business was operating just outside the city of Oakbrook, where she had been living for the past twenty years. She had raised her two children in Oakbrook, and as a family of three, they had been comfortable with their surroundings . . . until recently, that is.

Saralyn Green was approximately five feet seven inches tall, with a slim to average build. Her smile was a bit crooked, her eyes were hazel, and she had more "bad hair days" than good ones. She usually kept her ash blond hair at shoulder length and liked to wear baseball caps whenever the weather was rainy or very windy. Her skin was tanned from exposure to the summer sun. At forty-five years of age, Saralyn had been divorced twice.

Generally, her work wardrobe consisted of jeans or comfortable casual wear. Today however, Saralyn planned to meet friends later and had worn an ankle-length, sleeveless summer dress. The pale, sea green outfit was made out of a lightweight, fitted knit material; and she had added matching jewelry to complement the dress.

Saralyn was just about to make some morning coffee when the phone rang. As she reached for the receiver, she glanced at the pictures of family and friends scattered across her desk. These, of course, included several photographs of her two beautiful teenage daughters, of whom she was very proud. She smiled at the familiar faces.

The caller was Matthew Arboles confirming his 9:30 A.M. appointment.

"Yes, we are still scheduled for your interview." Then Saralyn added, "Yes, I look forward to meeting you also. Thank you for calling."

He has a nice voice, and he sounds reasonably professional, she thought. Matthew's call reminded Saralyn of something else: *I must get those résumés in order before the candidates start showing up.*

Back to the coffee. The coffee station was located in the opposite corner from Saralyn's office and next to the restroom. Her entire office building was approximately three thousand square feet. It directly adjoined the loading/unloading dock and garage, which measured approximately six thousand square feet. The workers on the dock had their own coffee station, soda machine, and restroom.

The foreman knocked on her office door and limped in on his cast. Benjamin Packard had been with Saralyn as the recycling center's foreman from the beginning. They met when she first considered starting the business. She had visited a recycling center in a neighboring town where Benjamin worked. He'd been helpful and friendly, answering all of her questions. On her final visit, Saralyn left her telephone numbers with Benjamin, and she had taken down his number. Then several weeks later, he called her, wanting to know if she was going to need a supervising foreman. He helped establish the new business, and they had been together ever since.

Ben (as Saralyn called him most of the time) was a large, fifty-seven-year-old black man. His children all grown, he once proudly showed Saralyn a picture of his young grandchild. He rarely confided any information about the death of his wife. All Saralyn knew was that she died from cancer and had evidently lingered on for several years.

Ben's close-cut hair was only about thirty percent gray, and before he'd broken his leg, he could have passed for at least ten years younger than his age. Saralyn suspected that the injury bothered him greatly and was far more painful than he would let on or admit to. Since his fall several weeks earlier from a ladder in his garage at home, Ben had been looking tired and drawn. His leg had been broken in the accident, but unfortunately he'd had to wait many hours before having it attended to. Today he wore old, denim coveralls with one pant leg cut off above the knee, to accommodate the leg cast.

"How are you doing this morning, Ben?"

"Oh, I've been better. I've also been worse, but believe me, I am not too old for this job." He sounded just a little cranky this morning.

"Well, don't worry, Ben," she reassured him. "You are very valuable to me and to this recycling center. You're the one who knows the system, how it works, and how to keep it all running." She continued with a smile, "You are irreplaceable. You are fantastic. You're brilliant."

Ben interrupted her: "OK, OK, enough."

They laughed affectionately and had a quick morning meeting to discuss the day's activities. Saralyn briefed him on the job candidates. Ben didn't really want to be involved with the interview process for this particular opening, even though they had seriously considered bringing in someone before his accident.

"Now, remember, this new guy we're looking for is just going to be your assistant, Ben. Nothing more. Have you had any coffee yet this morning?"

"You bet," Ben nodded. "Long ago. Better get back out there. We have that big shipment of newspapers coming in soon from the *City Star*."

Ben limped back through the large double doors, that connected the office spaces with the shipping/receiving area.

Just then, the 8:45 appointment arrived at 9:00 A.M.—late and with an arrogant air. As he sauntered through the building, casually touching chairs and filing cabinets, his body language said, 'Look at me. I'm wonderful.' Candidate number one, Mr. Swimner, had an average build and height, thinning brown hair, and brown eyes. His age, judging by his appearance and the date he'd graduated from college, was likely early thirties. Though educationally qualified, it soon became obvious that he had zero experience in the recycling business. During his interview, he also wasted no time in explaining physical restrictions that would prevent him from standing too long, lifting too much, etc.

This job required physically hard work. The newspaper advertisement for the position clearly stated that the successful applicant would need to do some manual labor, including lifting, in addition to the administrative responsibilities.

As Saralyn was finishing the first interview, her 9:30 A.M. appointment, Mr. Arboles, arrived at least ten minutes early. He peered into the large windows and saw that Saralyn was meeting with someone.

Matthew Arboles appeared to be about six feet tall, and Saralyn made a mental note that he looked capable of lifting. *Hopefully, this candidate more fully understands the job specifications.*

Matthew knew it was a little early for his appointment, so he decided to walk past the office windows and head toward the garage area.

Saralyn finished up her interview with candidate number one and politely informed him that he would be notified of their decision by the end of the week.

Once Mr. Swimner was out the door, Ben walked in with Matthew. They both came in through the big, metal double doors, laughing about something.

"Ms. Saralyn Green, I would like to introduce you to Matthew Arboles. He is your next appointment, I believe." Ben continued, "Matt and I have already had our introductions and a little get-acquainted chat."

"Thank you, Ben. It's nice to meet you, Matthew. Please come into the conference room while I go get your résumé from my office."

As Saralyn gathered her paperwork together, she mentioned where the coffee was located and suggested that he help himself. She had yet to have her first cup of the day and decided to get some now.

Matthew Arboles was rugged looking with light brown hair, hazel eyes, and a medium tan complexion. He looked to be in his mid-thirties.

After interviewer and interviewee settled into their seats in the conference room, the interview began.

"This coffee tastes so good. It's my first cup of the day. Are you sure you don't want any?"

"No, really. No thank you."

"So, Mr. Arboles, I see here that you are familiar with the area. You received your earlier education here and have just recently moved back."

As Saralyn was reviewing his résumé and application, she continued, "You have indicated that your last job reference is in Arizona. Was that your first experience with the workings of a recycling center?"

"Yes," Matt replied.

His voice is even warmer and more charming in person, Saralyn thought. Then she scolded herself. *Drink your coffee, wake up, and concentrate. Be professional!*

Matt was looking at her directly as he continued, "My job responsibilities were very similar to what the ad in the newspaper indicated you were looking for. Even though it was my first exposure to the recycling industry, I did work there for almost two years before they went out of business."

Saralyn curiously wondered out loud, "Do you know why they went out of business?"

Matt paused and thought for just a second. "No, I really don't know the details. I think it may have had something to do with the family owners wanting to retire. All of the employees were given only one day's notice. No warnings."

This information seemed a little strange to Saralyn. But she didn't dwell on it.

"I see, Mr. Arboles, that you graduated from the local junior college here in Oakbrook."

"Please, call me Matt," he requested gently.

"OK, Matt." Saralyn continued with only a slight pause, "How did you do with finance and statistics? Every now and then we may need whoever fills this position to be able to help out with the accounting matters, as well as the occasional heavy lifting."

"I can balance my checkbook," Matt laughed comfortably. "But seriously, I had my own tree-trimming business once, and I handled the books with no real problems that I can remember."

They continued to discuss some education and job experience specifics. Matt communicated well. He was articulate and convincing. Saralyn thanked him for coming and promised to notify him of her decision within two to three days, which would be no later than the end of the week.

Candidate number three was a no-show.

Between Mr. Swimner and Mr. Arboles, Saralyn had no trouble deciding to hire Matt. She then looked at the clock. It was already 10:00 A.M., and she hadn't gone over the orders and deliveries for the day. She reminded herself that she would need to finish these up quickly before leaving to meet her friends for lunch at the local mall.

After Matt had been gone for about forty-five minutes, Ben returned to Saralyn's office. "So, how did those interviews go?" He asked curiously.

Saralyn was guessing that he still felt his job might be in jeopardy if his leg didn't heal, even though she had reassured him several times that his job was very secure.

"Well, Ben, Mr. Swimner is not even an option. Looks like Matt is our best bet. He has the experience and education, and he indicated that a little lifting when necessary is no problem. What did you think of him?"

"Seemed fine to me," Ben responded.

"OK, Ben. Tomorrow, would you please call Mr. Swimner and notify him of our decision and then call Matt? Tell him he can start Monday if he's available. You will be responsible for the majority of his training."

"Sure thing, Ms. Green," Ben gave her a little wink. She noticed it, along with that sparkle in his eyes.

What was that all about? Saralyn wondered to herself. *Ben probably decided that Matt was the best candidate for this job before she had.*

"Oh, Ben, one more thing. I have that birthday lunch with friends at the Oaks Mall today. I may be back just a little late."

"OK, no problem. Just don't worry so much. We can manage the business for a couple of hours without you. Enjoy spending some time with your lady friends."

"I will, Ben. Thanks for everything. Try to stay off that leg now. I'll probably be leaving in an hour—after I finish this stack of paperwork."

As Saralyn poured herself another cup of coffee, she thanked God for watching over her business and for bringing Ben into her life. Ever since they'd first decided to convert these old abandoned brick buildings into a recycling center, Ben had secured her respect and trust.

The timing to open this business had been in their favor, since the city recently passed additional mandatory recycling codes. It had become necessary for all households to recycle a minimum of fifty percent of their garbage, and the city council voted steep fines into effect for people who didn't comply.

City residents had many new options available to them, one of which was "grasscycling"—simply leaving the finely cut grass clippings on the lawn after it had been mowed. This recycling measure extended the life of landfills and conserved water. Saralyn had learned of other benefits to grasscycling: it increased the biological activity near the soil's surface, recycled a natural resource, and resulted in a healthier lawn.

The Oakbrook Recycling Center accepted plastic, metal, tin, aluminum, newspaper, cardboard, copy or computer paper, and glass bottles and jars. City residents simply had to make sure they put their recyclables in the bright green containers, instead of in the single, black trash can each residence was now allotted.

Then, the large recycling disposal trucks brought their contents daily to the center from residential areas. Whereas, the local newspaper's main office and other companies had recycled materials picked up once a week.

Saralyn also transacted business with the public school district; several private schools, including one university; a dozen or so of the large corporate businesses around the city; plus dozens of smaller businesses. In turn, the Oakbrook Recycling Center separated the materials, which were then picked up by businesses who manufactured and marketed products produced from recycled materials.

Several times a year, Saralyn lectured in the schools. Her speaking engagements were mainly with elementary school classes. The primary purpose of these talks was to get kids thinking about the environment at an early age.

Saralyn believed in her business, and she no longer minded getting up in the morning to go to work. Her social life may not be perfect, but she had family and friends whom she loved dearly.

Oakbrook was a lovely place to live—a place where the harsh realities of crime and poverty were somewhat far removed and were usually only seen on the evening news. Located approximately seventy-five miles north of Los Angeles, the town had a half-dozen or so smaller neighborhood parks and several larger ones. As its name indicated, the town had many beautiful oak trees and several brooks running through the bigger parks. There was one main library and a number of bookstores.

Saralyn had been born and raised in Southern California and lived in Oakbrook almost half of her life. Her children grew up in Oakbrook. While Saralyn never left her doors unlocked—as she'd heard of some people doing in the Midwest—she never really worried about somebody breaking into her home or business either.

Completely unaware of the strange events about to take place, her family and friends soon would be caught off guard. They had never had to concern themselves with thoughts of someone watching them— until now that is.

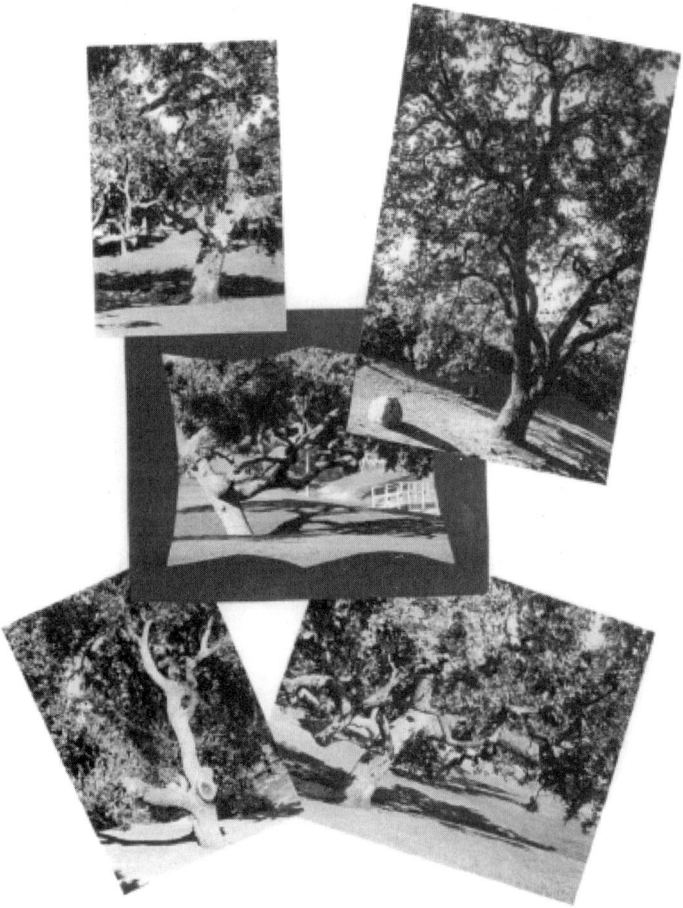

Chapter Two

On the short drive over to the mall, approximately two to three miles from her office, Saralyn had an opportunity to think about the friends she was about to meet for lunch. They all managed to survive working in a stressful corporate environment, and this eventually became a bond between them. They had been meeting for birthday lunches for almost nine years now, and they always got together for Christmas.

First, there was CC—Coral Cathleen Gateway. She was Saralyn's best friend. Black, forty-seven years old, and roughly the same height as Saralyn, CC also ran a business now, though she didn't own it. She was manager of a children's welfare and placement center and recently had been forced to deal with some tighter controls, since her agency was subsidized by government funds. She was divorced, and her one child, Eddie Jr., was grown and out on his own.

Eddie Jr., had spent four years in the United States Air Force and was now interested in continuing a career in communications. He still held an active secret security clearance and worked at the local military base as a civil service information technician, upgrading computer systems.

Eddie's father, CC's first husband, Edward Lincoln Jefferson Sr., had committed suicide after years of drug and alcohol abuse. CC's second marriage ended in divorce, as had Saralyn's two marriages.

Next there was Keri Lamb, a white, slightly overweight woman with thick, beautiful, shoulder-length hair, which she kept tinted a dark red shade. Recently, at their last birthday lunch, Keri turned fifty. She had been going through a divorce and was frequently on a diet. Keri blamed herself for her failed marriage, but honestly, Saralyn considered Keri's husband, George, a jerk. He left Keri, even though he was the one who'd had more than one affair. George was balding and not in great shape, but he believed he could do better than his current wife. Sometimes Keri admitted to still believing that if only she tried harder, George might come back. She hadn't talked about the situation as much lately, and Saralyn made a mental note to remember to ask Keri how she was doing.

Keri was sweet and always tried to please everyone. She had three children still at home—two in high school and one who'd recently started junior college. Lately, Keri also worried a lot about their family finances. She was the only one in their group who still worked for the same company—where they had all first met. Keri, however, had transferred long ago into a different department.

Deborah Kingsville was also in their group. In her late forties and black, Deborah was currently working as a paralegal for one of Oakbrook's larger law firms.

She had been securely and happily married for many years. Brad, her husband, was now doing some radio broadcasting for a local station. Previously he had been some kind of semi-pro athlete. Saralyn had always thought that Deborah and Brad made such an attractive couple. They were openly kind and affectionate toward each other. They were both Christians, and they had a classiness all their own. They had been leading a once-a-week Bible study in their home for several other married couples.

Deborah and Brad had had two children. Their son, William, had been accidentally shot and killed years ago, before Saralyn met Deborah. He was a good boy, according to Deborah, but he had been spending time with a couple of friends who had older brothers that lived in a crime-ridden neighborhood. The authorities suspected that the shooting may have been gang related. Unfortunately, William's homicide had never been solved.

It was because of their tragic experience that Brad wanted to move his family farther away from congested downtown Los Angeles. Their daughter, Monique, was in college and a good student motivated to do well. Saralyn had met her several times over the years.

Wendy Nielson was part of their group. *Well*, Saralyn thought to herself, *Wendy is a character*. At about five feet five inches, physically fit, and with short, extremely blond hair, Wendy was attractive in a Barbie-doll sort of way. She was in her mid-forties, divorced, never had children, and was always flirting. She dated a lot and frequently wanted to fix up the singles in the lunch group with dates. CC and Saralyn were often her target. Wendy, wasn't really careful about questioning the character of the men she dated and thought the other women were too discriminating. She worked for a plastic surgeon.

Lately Saralyn had been concerned about some of the new friends in Wendy's life, people who had been discussing alternative religions with her. These so-called New Age groups were growing and gaining in popularity. Their platform of beliefs, such as reincarnation, tolerance toward all types of worship, and the we-are-all-gods concept, had grown in popularity as well.

Today, they were all celebrating Wendy's and CC's August birthdays at one of their favorite restaurants in the local mall.

The restaurant was designed like an old-fashioned '50s diner with booths, onion rings, malts, etc. It always had been fun occasionally to splurge and eat there. Some went off their diets, and some ate veggie burgers.

Saralyn finally found a parking space. Next to the Christmas season, when the large lots were packed to overflowing, it was very difficult to find a space to park. Lunch crowds made the place so busy. It seemed even worse than usual today. She noticed the shuttle bus, but wasn't that far from the main entrance, so she decided simply to walk.

They had agreed to meet at around noon, and all arrived about the same time. Everyone, that is, except Wendy, who liked to make an entrance. There were hello hugs between each of the friends.

"Let's sit down ladies and think about what goodies we're going to eat, shall we?" Deborah suggested.

Saralyn laughed "Deborah, you are one classy woman. I like the way you enjoy thinking about your food."

As they sat down and menus were distributed, Keri asked, "Where is Wendy?"

CC responded, "Oh, you know, girlfriend, she'll be here." Looking up toward the waiter she informed him, "We'll be needing one extra menu, please."

Just as they were about to order, in walked Wendy.

More hugs and hellos.

"So, how is everyone? Have you all ordered yet?" Wendy asked.

"No, we were just about to," Saralyn answered as she gave a knowing look to CC, regarding Wendy's late entrance.

"Keri, why don't you go first. You'll need to get back to work the soonest."

Keri was ready. "I'm going to splurge today." And to the waiter, who had just stepped back up to their table and was waiting patiently, she said, "Let me have one of your special burgers, fries, and a chocolate malt."

Deborah ordered next. "Well, you know I'm going to have to order the exact same thing. It sounds so good."

While Wendy was still looking over the menu, Saralyn asked, "OK, CC, you're one of the birthday girls; what are you going to have?"

CC looked up toward the young waiter, "I'll have the chicken breast burger, small fries, and an ice tea." She added with a look back to the group, "I'm splurging a little too."

"Wellllll, I've decided to have today's special salad with light dressing and . . . hmm, a diet cherry cola," Wendy informed the waiter.

Saralyn ordered a cherry cola too, as well as a chicken breast burger and fries. Then she decided to add an order of onion rings to share with everyone.

As the waiter walked away to put in their order, everyone began talking and visiting at once.

"What's the story with only one entrance to this place?" Deborah asked. "I knew there had been some remodeling going on, but how long have those security guards been checking everyone at the door?"

Everyone else seemed just as curious about the recent changes.

Deborah continued, "I didn't know they were closing the other entrances. It's kind of like being at the airport."

"I know. If it hadn't been for Marissa, I wouldn't have known about those new little shuttle buses," Saralyn said, then added, "You know, she's still working at the Lotions 'n' Lipsticks store upstairs. The buses travel around the mall approximately every five minutes from the surrounding parking area. Marissa also mentioned a cute, new security guard, so I'll have to be checking him out. Anyway, she said the security checks started last week."

"I think all this… well… it's close to infringement on our rights or something," Wendy said. "What are they looking for anyway, weapons?"

"Could be," CC guessed.

Keri looked down anxiously at her watch to check the time. "I don't know. Maybe it's not such a bad thing. If it helps to control the gangs and drugs, maybe it's a good thing."

Another knowing glance was exchanged between Saralyn and CC as if to say, *What huge crime problem? In this sleepy town's mall!*

And Deborah wondered out loud, "What gangs? We don't really have a big problem out here. At least, nothing significant that I've heard of—not like the bigger cities. Last time I heard, Oakbrook had just hit the seventy-five thousand population mark."

"Hey, CC and Wendy," Saralyn prompted, "you'd better open some of your birthday gifts before they bring our food. Here, you can open mine first."

Saralyn handed each of them a birthday bag, beautifully decorated with ribbons tying the two handles together at the top. Deborah and Keri also brought out their gifts. CC and Wendy exchanged gifts with one another, and soon wrapping and ribbons covered the table.

After CC had finished opening her presents, she sincerely thanked everyone. "Saralyn, my friend, you know I love this body lotion and bubble bath. I've heard of this new scent of aromatherapy, but I haven't had a chance to try it yet." CC turned toward the others and genuinely thanked each of them for their gifts.

There were some unique candles, a scarf with matching pin, a gift certificate for the mall, and a pair of earrings. Wendy said her thank yous for similar gifts, and carefully they all started folding up the reusable gift bags and packing away the ribbons with the bows.

Just in time too. All the gifts were opened, fussed over, and put away just as the food arrived. During the meal, there was lighthearted teasing aimed toward Saralyn about getting to work with all men. (This included her brother Andrew, a part-time accountant, who came in once a week. Lately, however, he had been at the recycling center with increasing irregularity.)

Deborah thanked God for taste buds. Then CC added, "Yes, praise God for special friends too."

They all asked each other for updates on how family members were doing. Saralyn spoke about her two daughters, Marissa and Breanne. CC told them about some of the babies at the agency. Keri shared that her children were doing just fine, and Wendy talked about her latest boyfriend.

As they were finishing, Wendy, between the last bites of her salad, mentioned, "So, Saralyn, I've got someone I think you would really like to meet. How about it? Maybe a foursome for dinner some evening soon."

"Wendy, you know, Daniel and I still kind of have a near-date thing going on."

"What does that mean anyway—*a near-date thing*?" Keri asked.

Saralyn tried to explain, "Well, Daniel and I have been friends for about six months, and we're not seriously involved, but we're sort of more than just friends."

Deborah rolled her eyes upward. "Oh yes, that explains everything."

Keri looked at her watch again and regretfully said, "I'd better be getting back."

Saralyn remembered to quietly ask, "How are you doing, Keri? Seriously."

"Fine, really," Keri replied, as she stood up to leave after checking the bill and putting enough money down on the table to cover her share of the meal.

Everyone hugged Keri goodbye, and Saralyn made a mental note to call her for a more private conversation. She seemed unusually quiet and anxious today, kind of sad.

"Saralyn, I want to hear more about this new thirty-something-year-old man you hired this morning to help out at the recycling center," CC said. "What is he like?"

Wendy was suddenly more interested. "You hired someone new at the recycling center? Tell us about him. Is he married?"

"OK, ladies, there's nothing to tell. I really know very little about him, except what's on his résumé," Saralyn told them.

As they were chuckling, Saralyn suggested, "I think it's about time I head back to work as well. How much do I owe on this bill?"

The four remaining friends in turn checked out their lunch bill. When they were satisfied that enough had been chipped in for the meal, plus a tip, they said goodbye to their waiter and walked out of the restaurant into the main mall.

As the women started moving toward the only exit, they discussed the new security controls. It appeared that three guards were on duty at all times—two of them checking shoppers entering the mall, and a third checking everyone leaving. The search process was a basic slow walk through a detection door. If buzzers went off, the guards figured out what the person was wearing or carrying that had caused the alert. There were also new surveillance cameras located here and there in corners of the ceiling overhead.

That was the first time they all noticed the woman standing on the second floor. She was visible through the railing and was apparently watching everyone. After giving their group a quick glance, she looked toward one of the larger department stores. She was dressed in an attractive white and tan suit with a gray jacket. The jacket resembled a lightweight lab coat.

The woman's hair was pulled back into a neat bun, and she appeared to be in her mid- to late thirties.

"Who do you think that woman is?" CC asked as she leaned closer to Saralyn, gave her elbow a gentle nudge, and with her eyes gestured upward.

Wendy commented, "She acts like she's trying to look like someone official." Sarcastically, Wendy continued, "What kind of a fashion statement is she trying to make with that gray coat anyway? It's ninety degrees outside!"

Deborah offered an explanation: "Maybe she's some type of new mall manager overlooking the added security measures."

"I've never seen her before. I'll check with Marissa and see if she knows anything," Saralyn offered. "I have to come back here over the weekend to shop for Breanne. There's a modified dress code at the high school, so she needs some things. I'll let you all know if I see her again."

The ladies said more goodbyes, with hugs all around. As Wendy walked away toward her car, CC, Saralyn, and Deborah shouted after her, "See you next month or next birthday!"

Then, CC announced a prediction for Saralyn. "I'll bet, Wendy calls you soon about that foursome she wants you to go on."

Saralyn laughed. "I'll call you tomorrow, CC. Bye, Deborah. See you soon."

Chapter Three

"Mom, look at this; and it's on sale." Breanne had found a plain T-shirt she liked.

It was Saturday, mid-afternoon, and Saralyn had brought Breanne to a few of her favorite stores at the mall to shop for school clothes.

"I hate this new dress code," Breanne complained. Saralyn's youngest daughter seldom had a difficult time expressing her opinions. Breanne was a pretty teenager with long, light brown hair, hazel blue eyes, and stands approximately five-feet-six-inches. (Saralyn was fairly certain, however, that Breanne was still growing and would probably grow at least another inch or two.)

Saralyn tried to encourage her daughter: "I know, honey. Just remember, this is your senior year. Only one more year of high school!"

"Well," Breanne sighed loudly, "the pairs of nice pants I got last Christmas still fit fine. Maybe we can look for a long skirt or two. I still need to find some new blue jeans because both pairs at home have holes in the knees."

Then she added, a bit angrily, "I don't understand why we can't have some little hole that probably no one can see."

"It doesn't accomplish anything to get upset about it, Breanne. I told you, we can iron on a few of those small patches the school newsletter was talking about—the ones that are acceptable for the dress code."

"Mom, paaaaaaleeease!" Breanne protested. "You know I won't wear some silly patch! Here's a pair, Mom. I'm going to go try these on now." She carried a pair of jeans toward the dressing rooms with the other clothes she'd found to try on.

Saralyn decided to browse around a little. She had seen one or two cute tops she liked, but then she decided she didn't want to hassle with trying them on. It was not her favorite thing to do—strip down in a dressing room under all those unflattering lights. (It was an aversion she shared with several of her friends.) Rather than subject herself to the unpleasant procedure, Saralyn frequently purchased clothing and later returned it if it didn't fit; she definitely preferred trying on new garments in the comfort of her own home.

Saralyn stayed close by the dressing rooms, waiting for Breanne and watching, out of the corner of her eye, for any odd-looking individuals in gray lab coats. Once Breanne had finished, it was just about time to leave or they would be late meeting Marissa.

"OK, Breanne. Let's go stand in line and pay for these. I told your sister we would meet for a snack at the food court downstairs during her break."

"Thank you, Mom, for the new jeans and stuff," Breanne nicely said as they headed out of the store.

Saralyn gently put her arm around Breanne's shoulder. "You're welcome, honey. I'm just happy you found a few things you like. The clothes fit and satisfy the new dress code requirements too."

"Let's go downstairs here, beautiful." Saralyn gestured in front of them as they reached the top of the escalator.

Sometimes, Breanne can be so sweet. It had been amazing for Saralyn to experience the amount of love a mother can have for her children. She had a tendency to use terms of endearment a lot when she talked to her daughters. Saralyn once read how important it was to do that in order to build self-esteem in your children.

Self-esteem was something she herself had all too frequently battled with in the past but not nearly as much anymore. Once Saralyn had started attending church on a more regular basis, she had received a better understanding of how each individual, through faith in Christ, becomes a new creation. A negative self-image can be difficult to move beyond. It takes inner strength not to worry about and relive the past. Saralyn had learned that everyone has bad stuff happen to them; it's how we react to the negative and whether or not we move on that is most important.

Saralyn realized that once a person is less obsessed with how awful they think they look on any particular day, the more at peace they become. She did not want her children to suffer the same struggles with self-doubt and inferiority complexes that she had faced. Besides, both daughters truly were absolutely beautiful as far as Saralyn was concerned. She enjoyed reminding them of it over and over again.

As Saralyn and Breanne were walking to meet Marissa, Breanne saw a friend from school. Nicky was an outgoing friend with whom Breanne had several classes the previous school year.

Today her outfit looked very similar to Breanne's. They were both wearing blue-jean shorts and pale-colored sleeveless tops made out of T-shirt material. Nicky also had long, brown hair, except hers was a little lighter than Breanne's. This day, they both wore the popular thin-strapped, thick-soled sandals.

The three of them stopped to talk briefly, in front of a greeting card store that had vacation posters with inviting beach scenes on display in its front windows.

All along the bottom of the posters were greeting cards with messages such as 'Wish you were here' and 'Bon voyage.'

Saralyn smiled at the girls as she listened in on their conversation.

"Hey, Nicky, did you get your schedule yet? What teacher do you have for history?"

"I think it's Mr. Darian," Nicky answered, and then added, "My brother stopped by the campus last week with a few of his friends, and he said there's some new, big lockers there. They couldn't figure out how to open them. The lockers have no combination locks, and there is no place for a padlock. They're like some high tech mystery or something."

"I wonder who will get stuck with the old smaller lockers. Hopefully, just the freshmen and sophmores," Breanne pondered.

"Isn't this new dress code stuff weird?" Nicky asked. "No holes in our blue jeans. No writing on our T-shirts or sweatshirts!"

"Yeah, really, and after the first five days of school, they can suspend you for a day for not wearing the right clothes." Breanne then asked, "So, Nicky, did you have fun on vacation with your dad?"

"Yeah, we drove up the coast and stopped off at a bunch of places. Hearst Castle was kind of neat and so was the Monterey Bay Aquarium."

Breanne shared her memories of the aquarium. "A few years ago, when my mom and I took a trip up the coast like yours, we stayed at bed-and-breakfast places. I remember the aquarium. The sea otters would float on their backs while they were eating or napping. They looked so cute!"

"Well, wish I could have taken a friend. But then, I guess my dad and I wouldn't have spent as much time together. I think he misses seeing me and being involved in the everyday stuff. I guess I sometimes miss him too. Anyway, what about you, Breanne? Where did you go this summer?"

"Well, we didn't go away for any long vacations. We took some day trips to the beach." Then, Breanne complained, "I can't believe that now we also have to wait until we're seventeen or graduated before getting a driver's license. Hey, Nicky, isn't your birthday like right after school starts?"

"Yeah, it's September 29, and I'll be seventeen. I still can't believe I'll finally be able to get my driver's license."

"My birthday isn't until late November," Breanne commiserated further. "I still have to wait for months."

"Well, girls, time goes by so fast, you'll both be driving around town before you know it," Saralyn interjected. "Besides, this way you can concentrate more on homework and studying."

Both girls moaned.

"Let's get going, Breanne. We're running a little late. Good to see you again, Nicky."

Just as Saralyn and Breanne reached the food court, found a vacant table, and sat down, Marissa joined them. Saralyn's oldest daughter was also a pretty teenager. At nineteen, she was almost no longer a teenager, but a young adult. Marissa had shoulder-length, ash blond hair with lighter blond streaks throughout. Her eyes were blue, and she was about five feet six inches tall.

Marissa had been working at Lotions 'n' Lipsticks for almost six months and was getting tired of it. The store's dress code included having to wear an apron-looking vest boldly imprinted with the company's trademark emblem and the words LOTIONS 'N' LIPSTICKS.

"Hi, honey. Sit down here." Saralyn motioned for her older daughter to sit next to her. "What does everyone want to drink?"

As they ordered lemonades, pretzels, and one root beer float to share, Saralyn asked, "So, Marissa, is anyone talking about the new security procedures?"

"Yeah, that's pretty strange." Breanne commented.

As Marissa gave Breanne one of those who's-talking-to-you-anyway kind of looks, she answered her mom: "No, I guess people are getting used to it. I saw and spoke to that new security guard again today. He seems nice."

"Soooooo, is he cute? How old is he? Where did he go to school?" Breanne asked curiously, teasing her sister.

Marissa breathed deeply and sighed a long why-am-I-the-big-sister kind of sighs. "None of your business."

"I suppose the security checkpoint is no big deal," Breanne concluded. "Mom, do we have time to look for shoes?"

"Well," Saralyn reminded her daughters, "I'm meeting Daniel tonight for dinner." She decided to add, "We might have half an hour or so left."

Marissa and Breanne exchanged a sour look. Neither one really liked Daniel much. When asked why, they both said they couldn't put their finger on the exact reasons. Saralyn believed that they just had trouble with their mom dating anyone.

"Are you still having these near-date experiences?" Marissa teased.

"You know they're not really dates, but Daniel does seem to be a good man." Then Saralyn changed the subject. "Boy, the mall is busy today. Hey, honey, have you seen any new managers around the mall?" Saralyn had forgotten to ask

Marissa about the woman in the gray jacket until now. "I know this sounds a little strange, but is there a woman who looks kind of official, wearing a knee-length gray jacket?"

"Yep. As a matter of fact, the girls at the store and I were talking about her today, and about that other guy. We were wondering who they were. They both seemed to be monitoring something. Maybe, they're involved with the new security stuff."

"Other guy? What other guy?" Saralyn quickly asked.

"There's this man who's here some of the time too, and he wears that same kind of jacket. We saw the two of them talking yesterday."

"Hmm."

"Well, thanks for the lemonade and pretzel, Mom. I'd better be getting back. Break time is over."

"OK, beautiful," Saralyn patted Marissa on the hand briefly. "I'll be gone before you get home tonight. Are you going out later?"

Marissa nodded. "I don't exactly know the details yet. We'll probably make plans at the last minute."

"As usual," Breanne added.

This time Saralyn gave her a stern look.

"Well, if you do, please don't stay out real late. I would love for you to come to church with us tomorrow. Late service doesn't start until 10:30 A.M. you know."

"I know, Mom, but don't count on it. Bye. Have fun on your near-date or whatever you want to call it."

Saralyn called after her, "Bye, Marissa. Be sure you have someone walk out with you tonight, since it will be dark when you get off work."

"I will, Mom. Don't worry. See ya later."

Chapter Four

Daniel was standing near the entrance to the restaurant when Saralyn arrived. "I'm not quite certain why you still insist on meeting me places. You know it's no big deal for me to swing by your place and pick you up."

"I know, Daniel. It's just, well . . . Hey, you drove us to that brunch a couple of weeks ago."

Daniel shook his head slightly as they both followed the hostess who led them to their table.

Saralyn was wearing tapered, beige-colored slacks and a white blouse with sheer short sleeves. Her open-toed, white, slip-on sandals were stylish and softly comfortable; sometimes, though, they had a tendency to slide off of her feet while walking. She tripped unnoticeably as they sat.

"Italian food is one of my favorites," Saralyn said.

They made small talk as they scanned the menus.

"How is your sister Marcy doing?" Saralyn asked.

"Oh, she's doing much better," Daniel replied. "You know, she will never be a surgeon. Her fingers will always be a little stiff. Luckily, she'll be able to continue practicing medicine. In fact, Marcy just recently told me that she's thinking about working for that new government medical clinic. I don't really know any of the details."

"Is that the new group of government employees who recently started working in CC's building?"

"Could be. I don't know."

"Well, thank God the burns on her hands have healed. It's amazing now what can be done with plastic surgery. Did I mention that Wendy, one of the women I met for lunch the other day, is working for a plastic surgeon?"

"You might have," Daniel replied. "I really don't know which doctors Marcy has gone to. She says the physical rehabilitation therapy treatments will continue indefinitely." Then he asked, "How are your girls?"

Saralyn shared the latest news of what had been going on in her daughters' lives. "Marissa just received a small raise at work, and Breanne is pretty much ready to start school next week."

The waiter came back to their table, ready to take the order. Saralyn spoke first, "I know exactly what I'm having. The usual." She laughed softly to herself and continued. "I'll have the angel-hair pasta with sun-dried tomatoes, basil, onions, and lots of garlic. No cheese on anything and no mushrooms. I'll also have a small side salad with light Italian dressing."

Daniel ordered a house special, linguini with clam sauce, and a side salad. Both ordered a small glass of wine to be brought with their dinner. Just when they had finished ordering, Daniel excused himself to go to the restroom.

As she watched him walk away and while he was gone, Saralyn attempted to analyze Daniel. They had known each other for about six months now, and at times, he could be charming.

They met at a singles' group that Saralyn had visited a few times. The group met regularly at the church where Daniel was an elder; he had been a member of that church for many years.

Daniel was forty-nine years old and had dark brown hair. He had been losing his hair for years and was self-conscious about it. Most of the time, he kept the preoccupation with his hair and with himself hidden. He was about six feet tall, with an average build—not slim and not overly heavy either. He was not really into sports or keeping fit, and according to him, he only occasionally watched sporting events on TV.

Tonight Daniel was wearing a nice pair of brown slacks and a long-sleeved, light tan-colored cotton shirt. He often liked to roll up the sleeves several times, almost to his elbows.

Saralyn thought that he looked especially handsome tonight. His shirt appeared to have been ironed. (Sometimes Daniel had a tendency to look a little rumpled.) She wondered if he had done the ironing himself or if he had taken the shirt to the cleaners. Then Saralyn caught herself: *Stop dwelling on such petty thoughts.*

Saralyn liked him. While looking around at the patrons dining throughout the restaurant, she recalled his telling her the story about his wife. The woman had left him several years ago after their marriage went bad, taking their son and moving to northern California.

Daniel had to move into a small apartment because so much of his money had been spent on attorney's fees, alimony, and child support. Saralyn sympathized with him and with his fight for visitation. According to him, everything had been his ex-wife's fault. But of course, Saralyn realized the ex-wife probably had a different story.

Daniel had also recently changed jobs. He was now working in a sales and marketing department for some growing biotechnology company. He was a little vague about what he had been doing previously, mostly the same type of sales. She didn't push for additional details either.

Saralyn believed Daniel was experiencing rough circumstances lately. So she sometimes ended up making excuses for him. She also found herself feeling sorry for him. He wasn't overly optimistic or flattering toward people; however, he paid her some attention. Before meeting him, she had occasionally missed receiving male affection. Saralyn was aware of being single in a couples' world.

It got lonely sometimes, especially at night.

When Daniel returned, Saralyn smiled at him warmly.

"So, when are you going to switch churches and start attending the one I go to?" Daniel asked, as he pulled out his chair and sat back down at their table.

"You know," Saralyn continued to smile, "I really love all the people and the pastor where I've been going. Besides, Breanne is happy going there too, and that's important."

Daniel took her hand and looked into her eyes. "I would just like to see you more often," he said romantically.

There was a part of her that thought, *Ah, how sweet*. However, her response was a little defensive. "Well, the Recycling Center has been very busy. I've even hired another manager to help Ben out. Business is booming, which is actually great! Since the city passed their new recycling ordinances, volume continues to increase."

For the moment, Daniel gave up trying to get intimate. Pretending to be curious, he asked, "What are the new ordinances?"

Saralyn explained briefly, "The city now requires that each and every household recycle 50% of their trash. There are additional fees, and even fines, if a household falls below the 50%. There are incentives and rate reductions if people use trash compactors and recycle more than 75%. For companies that follow stringent environmental standards, such as buying in bulk post-consumer recycled paper, there are special recognition awards."

The salads arrived, along with delicious looking garlic bread, warm from the oven. Good timing for Daniel. He was visibly starting to really lose interest, glancing away from Saralyn and allowing his gaze to wander around the restaurant.

Daniel didn't share Saralyn's enthusiasm and interest in ecology issues, or in education for that matter. He had not been particularly supportive whenever she mentioned furthering her education by going back to school to earn a graduate degree. Daniel thought that she should be more submissive to him, spending her time figuring out what would make him happy. Of course, he never would have come right out and admitted to the latter.

Saralyn spoke softly after the waiter placed their salad plates in front of them and had walked away, "You know, of course, I don't place the recycling business or education above God. He created absolutely everything. While we are here on earth, though, I strongly believe common sense is important. Everyone should be aware of and contribute to taking care of the environment."

Daniel was frequently concerned about what those around them would think. He looked around to see if anyone might have heard their conversation. The rest of their evening was spent enjoying the food. The waiter brought another basket of warm garlic bread along with their main course.

Saralyn thoroughly enjoyed her dinner. "I am so stuffed, and I loved every bite of it. I'll have to take the rest home with me. There's enough here for another whole meal!" Saralyn sighed heavily. "Did you enjoy your linguini?" she asked.

"It was good. They should have used a little more sauce, but it was OK."

"I'll be right back, Daniel." Saralyn stood up and turned toward the restroom.

Just then, the waiter arrived with a large tray of half a dozen desserts.

"No way could I eat anything more." She turned back toward Daniel, "If you want to order something, I'll just have a bite of yours."

After several minutes, Saralyn exited the restroom and jumped, startled. Daniel was waiting awkwardly for her just outside the door. *Guess we're not going to be having any dessert,* she thought. He was smiling tentatively, and suggested that they continue the evening by going somewhere else for coffee.

"No, thank you, Daniel. I have really enjoyed our dinner. But, you know Breanne is at home alone. Even though I know she's fine and I can trust her, I just want to make sure everything is OK."

Saralyn was making excuses. She knew Breanne would be fine, but she really did not want to spend any more time with Daniel. "Besides, I know you have to get up early tomorrow morning to attend your elders' meeting before church services start."

Daniel walked Saralyn to her car. The late August night was still warm.

"It's really very beautiful out tonight, isn't it?" Saralyn looked up toward the sky. "It's so clear; look at all the stars."

As they arrived at her car, she reached up to give him a friendly hug, and he kissed her gently on the cheek. Then his arms tightened around her. When his hug became more demanding and he tried forcefully to lock lips, she pulled away.

"Thank you very much for dinner, Daniel. It's my turn to pick up the check next time." Saralyn was breathless with surprise and wanted to leave quickly.

"Goodnight. I'll call you." Daniel said a little impatiently, as Saralyn climbed into her car. She closed the door and busied herself with the car keys and seatbelt. He watched her drive away.

What is wrong with me? Saralyn asked herself. *Here's a perfectly good opportunity to enjoy spending time with a man. He's someone I actually like spending time with, but I just don't want to spend too much time with him. Confusing! Why are my feelings for him so confused? There is something about Daniel that just doesn't seem quite sincere.*

During her drive home, she recalled a recent conversation with CC. They had been talking about Daniel, and Saralyn was trying to explain her feelings for him—or more accurately, the lack of deeper more intimate feelings.

She told CC that she liked Daniel and maybe even felt love for him as a friend. When it came to being in love, however, those deeper feelings of intimacy just weren't there.

It might be just the male friendship that I enjoy. Could it be that a stronger, more passionate, crazy, and all-consuming kind of love only happens once in our lives! Saralyn wondered. She had felt that way twenty years ago, and not since. Even so, she discovered later that the object of her affections lied to her about many things. Their relationship had been built on deceit.

Saralyn had asked CC for her opinion and advice. Did CC think it possible that a person's ability to love might lessen over the years, perhaps as a result of a broken heart or feelings of being used. CC understood Saralyn's numbness. Sometimes, people can be emotionally drained and prefer not to lower their protective shields. However, CC just figured that Saralyn hadn't met the right man. According to CC, apparently there was a statistically verifiable lack of eligible men in their town.

CC suggested that the ability to love did not lose its integrity like recycled paper did.

She used an analogy with which Saralyn could identify: after a piece of paper has been used and recycled, used and recycled, there is a point where that piece of paper eventually loses its original strength, because its fibers have broken down into shorter fibers. Paper can be recycled only a finite number of times. Also, that recycled paper can't be made as white as it once was without harmful chemicals.

Love was so different. Love was infinite.

CC knew Scripture well—probably even better than Daniel knew it. She had mentioned to Saralyn that some people seem capable only of "talkin' the talk" and found it much harder when it came time for them to be "walkin' the walk."

Saralyn's friend had reminded her that we are all human and sometimes it is difficult to trust again. The Bible has taught us to trust those who have proven themselves trustworthy, not just to trust because that person has asked you to trust them and to believe in them. She reminded Saralyn, that Christians don't necessarily have to accept it blindly when another person professes to be a Christian. We are also to be "wise as serpents."

Chapter Five

The music director led the congregational singing in the Sunday morning church service. Saralyn thought back to the conversation she'd had with Breanne in the car on the way over.

"Why don't you force Marissa to come to church with us, Mom?" Breanne had asked in frustration. "You should make her come with us. Tell her it's very important to you."

After taking a deep breath and letting it out slowly with a sigh, Saralyn responded, "Well, honey, I did. When I went in to wake her up, I even said 'please.' Above all Breanne, it's important to Marissa's own personal relationship with God. We need to pray she'll understand that soon."

As Saralyn focused back on the music, she looked around the now-familiar church sanctuary. The white walls appeared to be constructed of large bricks. The building had high vaulted ceilings, with one section of floor-to-ceiling windows located at the front of the church. There were rows of seats divided in four sections. The floor had a gradual incline from the front to the back. Toward the front wall and facing the congregation stood a large, wooden cross that must have been a minimum of eighteen feet tall. On the side walls were beautiful banners that were around six feet high and four feet wide; they were imprinted with such words as REJOICE, HE IS RISEN, and AMAZING GRACE, in large block letters.

I love it here, Saralyn thought. *I love the music. I love the singing.* Saralyn couldn't sing a note on key and was actually rather tone deaf. The good news for her was that even with no musical talent, her praises sounded lovely to God.

The familiar music, familiar surroundings—how lucky we all are. Unfortunately, this basic freedom we have is slowly being taken away. There has been an unusual and destructive trend of government hostility toward religious expression. Saralyn was up on her mental soapbox now.

The people's right to pray has been taken away from individuals while they are on public property; this includes schools. The government has had a difficult time in reaching balanced, common-sense decisions. If someone wants the right to pray or to recognize their religion, they should be allowed to do so, within reason.

Saralyn continued in her thoughts. *This freedom is such a basic one—one upon which our country was originally founded. If, on the other hand, opponents to religious rights in public places feel their rights are being violated, they simply can choose not to participate. It's an individual's decision. No public or school official need enforce or take away that right. How fortunate American citizens are to still have the freedom to worship at church.*

Just then she saw him. There was a man sitting in the back of the church. She had never seen him before. He was wearing nice slacks, a white shirt with a tie, and *a knee-length gray coat.*

How bizarre. Saralyn tried not to stare. Besides, she had to twist herself a bit too far in her seat just to see him. *How strange,* she thought, *that he would be wearing the same kind of coat as the woman at the shopping mall.*

What was he doing here? Could he be some governmental representative? Years earlier, Saralyn remembered taking a drive to a church nearer the LA area. She had gone there with Marissa and CC, while Breanne spent the weekend with her dad.

There had been a high-ranking political figure who attended church there with his wife. Right before the church service was to start, these secret service bodyguards wearing their dark suits, earphones, and sunglasses walked in. After they had secured the area, the high-ranking official and his wife entered the sanctuary, and all of them sat down in the pews across from Marissa.

Saralyn remembered that day well, not only because of the unusual secret service experience but also because after church they had all gone to brunch on the beach. They were then treated to a show of graceful dolphins dancing across the ocean, viewed through the big restaurant windows. Quite a memorable day.

Maybe that's who this man sitting in the back of the church is—some kind of secret service agent. However, he appeared to be alone.

Saralyn settled in next to Breanne to listen to Pastor Dave's sermon. This morning he was teaching from the New Testament, highlighting passages from the Gospel of John. These verses of scripture contained some basic instruction on how to obtain everlasting life. From the text, it was clear that there was only one true way to make it into heaven!

Pastor Dave had a pleasant, strong voice. He had wanted to be a preacher for as long as he could remember. Having grown up knowing God as personal Lord and Savior, David Lawson long desired to share this truth with everyone.

Saralyn and the others in her singles' group, had an opportunity to get to know him over the past year and a half—ever since he started leading their Bible study on Thursday nights. Pastor Dave, as most of the congregation now called him, was about five feet eleven inches tall, with brown hair, brown eyes and a great smile. He was in his mid-forties and was raising two young children on his own. His wife died years earlier from complications during childbirth, shortly after the birth of their youngest, Teressa, who was now nine. The oldest boy, Trevor, was about eleven. Saralyn once had asked someone what the complications were. She was told it involved an aneurysm of some kind.

Pastor Dave taught his sermons with zestful character and personality. Today, he explained how John, whom Jesus loved, wrote about God's love for everyone. God sent His Son into the world not to condemn it, but so that people who believe could have everlasting life through Him.

After the sermon and during the announcements, Pastor Dave asked for any newcomers to raise their hands so the ushers could hand them a welcome packet full of church information. Saralyn twisted slightly; she wanted to see if the stranger in the back raised his hand. He hadn't.

After the service ended, Breanne went over to check out the refreshment table for a few minutes. She knew that her mom liked to visit with her friends from the Thursday night single adults Bible study. Several members from the group gathered just outside the main church entrance.

"Have any of you seen that gentleman before?" Saralyn asked curiously, just as the stranger walked out the door.

As most everyone shook their heads, indicating they hadn't, Liz, a woman who was about Saralyn's age, answered quietly,

"I don't think I have, why do you ask?"

"Oh, it may be nothing. That's kind of an unusual coat to be wearing, though, don't you think? Especially for summer."

The man was standing just outside the main doors, casually looking around. As he took a look at his watch, he walked toward the parking lot.

Saralyn watched him for several minutes until he got into his car. Then she decided to leave as well and catch up with Breanne, who had already gone to wait in the car. "Bye for now, everyone. Have a good week. Hope to see you all at Bible study."

"Bye, Saralyn. You're not going to brunch with us today?" Liz asked.

"No, not today. Breanne and I have a ton of chores to do around the house, including piles of laundry," Saralyn explained.

"I'm glad I did mine yesterday," Liz teased.

"We should have too," Saralyn admitted to procrastinating. "Ah well, have a good week, Liz." Then Saralyn waved goodbye.

After most of the chores were done, Saralyn asked if Breanne would like to help trim the rosebushes.

"No thanks, Mom. Some friends and I want to go see a movie. Is it OK for me to go? I've done all the stuff you wanted me to. Can you drive at least one way?"

"Yes, I think I can probably manage that. Do you want me to sit next to you and your friends?" Saralyn said teasingly.

"Not today, Mom." Breanne seemed tired.

"Well you're not in a very good mood this afternoon. It was just a joke!"

"I'm not in a joking mood."

"OK, honey. Just let me know when you want to leave. I'm ready when you are."

Saralyn suspected, that Marissa and Breanne may have had another one of those you-get-away-with-more-than-I-do kinds of fights between sisters.

After Saralyn took Breanne and two of her friends to the movies, she had some time alone to work with the rosebushes.

Marissa was out, who knew where?

Among Saralyn's favorite roses was the Peace Rose—one of the most famous roses in the history of modern breeding. The petals change from pale ivory at the center to light yellow, and then to a touch of pink at the tips. This plant is extraordinarily hardy, and the flowers smell enchanting too. Unfortunately, however, the roses were not very fragrant this summer, since the days had been hot and dry. Having pruned the bushes way down earlier in the season, Saralyn feared they wouldn't grow back the same; but they did. In fact, they were fuller and stronger.

One of Saralyn's mom's favorite roses had been the Red Masterpiece. These roses were a beautiful, deep, dark red. Her mom also had loved the White Masterpiece. One flower had a heavy, old-fashioned rose scent, and the other a light and sweet smell.

Suddenly the phone rang and startled Saralyn, the loud noise intruding on the quiet of the afternoon.

"Hey, Saralyn. What are you up to?"

"Hi, Wendy. I'm just in the process of clipping some rosebushes."

"No kidding. You do gardening?"

"Yes. Actually, I love it. It can be therapeutic sometimes after a hectic week. How are you? What are you up to today?"

"Oh, me? I'm just fine. Remember at lunch I mentioned to you that there is this great guy I've met. Well, he has a friend, and I've told him all about you. He'd really like for us all to meet. Why don't the four of us get together and go 'clubbing' down in LA?"

"I don't think so, Wendy."

"Oh, come on. We can get all dressed up, and we might even meet some famous people in those downtown clubs. Let me tell you about Richard. He smokes only occasionally, and even though he and Jimmy are kind of like regulars at the Oakbrook Inn Bar, it's not like they're hanging out there every night. He's really good looking and kind of lonely. Come on, Saralyn. We could have some fun."

"Listen, Wendy, I really think not. Don't get me wrong, OK? I do appreciate your asking me and everything. But you know me. I don't like that club scene at all anymore—all those people getting drunk. It's been years!"

"Are you sure?"

"Yes, I'm sure. Thanks, but no thanks. Hey, Wendy, I do look forward to when we can all get together again for lunch. Soon, I hope. Have a good Sunday."

"OK, Saralyn. You'll probably be sorry. These are two great looking guys. See you at our next lunch."

As Saralyn hung up the phone, she made a mental note to give CC a call first thing tomorrow morning. She wanted to share with her friend about the stranger at church and this phone call from Wendy.

Chapter Six

Saralyn and CC spoke briefly on the telephone Monday morning and again on Wednesday. However, CC had several meetings for which she was preparing, and Saralyn had to deal with large shipments of material coming in from a new customer.

The friends didn't have a chance to get together until Friday, so they decided to meet for coffee at the recycling center Friday morning at around 9:45. CC would stop by between her business errands. In the meantime, Saralyn received two troubling phone calls: one was from Andrew, Saralyn's brother; the second—more damaging and memorable than the first—was from Daniel.

The phone call from Andrew came late Monday afternoon. Andrew lived approximately thirty-five to forty minutes from Oakbrook, in a city closer to Los Angeles. Always having been good with numbers, Andrew made a career of doing accountant-type work. In addition to his part-time work for a half-dozen other small businesses and doing IRS filings at tax time, Andrew had been working once a week at the recycling center for the past year now. He had called to let Saralyn know that he would not be able to make it to work for a week. He was going out of town, taking his new girlfriend, Sandy, to Hawaii.

"Thanks for letting me know, Andrew," Saralyn told him, though she was not crazy about the news. Invoices had started to pile high around the office. Until recently, keeping up with all the recycling center's financial paperwork had taken between six and eight hours a week. However, as the business grew, so had the bookkeeping chores.

But everyone deserves a vacation, Saralyn reminded herself. "So, where are you guys going in Hawaii?"

"It's some inexpensive package deal for the island of Oahu. Sandy's never been, so we'll have a good time no matter where we go."

"Well, don't forget to see Pearl Harbor, and both of you would probably love to go outrigger surfing on Waikiki Beach. The girls and I really had a lot of fun in those outrigger canoes when we were in Hawaii years ago."

"Got it. We'll remember. Hey, Sis, before I forget, guess who I saw at a party last week?"

"I have no clue. Who?"

"I hate to tell you this, but you deserve a fair warning."

"What is it, Andrew?"

"Well, it was Daniel. He was pretty wasted. It was a party at one of the local sports bars here in town. Sandy and I just stopped in to say hi to friends. He wasn't just drunk, I don't think. He practically didn't recognize me when I went up to him and said hi."

Saralyn inhaled deeply and exhaled slowly. "You know, Andrew. I guess I'm not really surprised."

"Saralyn, I think he might have been strung out on some of the new MADS. You know, those mind-altering, prescription psychotherapy drugs that a lot of people are abusing. He seemed real paranoid about seeing me there too, so don't tell him I told you."

"Don't worry about it. Anyway, I've already pretty much decided not to see him anymore. This just really confirms my suspicions. Daniel has seemed a lot more self-obsessed than usual lately."

"Well, I'd better get going. Sandy and I still have some more travel arrangements to make."

"Andrew, just one more thing. I wanted to let you know that there have been some unusual things happening around here lately."

Saralyn told her brother briefly about the individuals who had been showing up around Oakbrook in gray coats, plus about the new security measures at the mall. He told her not to worry and that she was probably reading too much into it.

"Well, Sis. Maybe you've been watching too much science fiction on TV lately. Technology is a great thing, Saralyn." Andrew tried to comfort her further.

"Just look at the new and improved computer bookkeeping programs we have access to nowadays—makes accounting incredibly faster."

"I know, Andrew." Then she warned, "Just be more aware and observant, would you? It's probably going on in your town too."

Daniel's telephone call was much more unpleasant. He called on Wednesday to ask her out for dinner over the weekend. Saralyn was kind, but firm.

"Daniel, I just don't think we are right for each other."

"What in the world are you talking about? We get along great! You just need to loosen up a little. Listen, nobody's perfect."

"I know that none of us is perfect, Daniel—really. I don't want anyone's feelings to get hurt here, but I'm telling you now that I don't want to see you anymore. Let's just try to part on friendly terms, OK?"

"You don't know how stupid you are!"

Stunned, Saralyn managed to say, "What? Excuse me?"

"I know what you're really thinking. You think you're better than I am." Daniel's tone had definitely changed. He sounded insulting. He kept talking as if he'd rehearsed his words. "Well, you're not anyone to brag home about. You should be thankful I wanted to be seen out in public with you at all."

His words had such a sting to them. Saralyn was hurt and angry. She wanted to end the conversation—to finish it quickly.

"OK, Daniel, this is ridiculous. There's no need to start throwing insults. It's time to officially stop seeing each other; it's that simple. Goodbye."

"Um, ah, I . . ."

Saralyn heard him trying to say something else as she hung up the telephone. She was hurt and confused, her self-image injured.

What happened to Daniel's Christian demeanor? Boy, is he ever showing his true colors. Well, CC was right about him being capable of only "talkin' the talk." Why didn't I see this side of him earlier? I'm certainly glad it's all over.

It wasn't over.

The next day, Daniel called again. He acted like everything between them was just fine. It was as if they had never spoken the day before.

Why is he calling me again? Saralyn was caught off guard.

Daniel began by saying, "I know we spoke briefly yesterday, but we probably didn't mean any of those things we said to each other."

"I meant what I said Daniel!"

Daniel continued as if he hadn't heard her, "You know, I think we can work out whatever minor differences we might have. You just need to listen more carefully."

"Me. I need to listen more carefully," Saralyn said flatly, sighing heavily. "Daniel, please. I'm at the point where I really don't even want to talk to you anymore, let alone go out with you. You were very insulting."

"Me? Really? I was tired. I didn't get a good night's sleep, and I had a headache." Daniel had a lot of excuses.

"Actually, our phone conversation is a little fuzzy. But, I'm sure I wouldn't have said anything too insulting. Listen, why don't we just start from scratch—wipe the slate clean, so to speak. We've both got a lot of issues to work on."

"Yes, I know, Daniel. No one is perfect. We discussed that yesterday."

"We did?"

"Yes, we did, and I meant what I said about not seeing each other anymore. I'm serious!" Saralyn's voice softened as she finished. "Please don't call me again, Daniel. There's not even a friendship to be salvaged here. Goodbye, and God bless."

Daniel began to ramble. He said she was no Christian or she would be nicer to him, more forgiving. He accused her of not being smart enough to figure out how to make him happy. If she were really a Christian, she could determine how to make their relationship work. As Saralyn decided once more just to hang up the phone, he was still rambling about how worthless she was.

Dear Lord, I hope I never hear from him again. The pressure of trying to maintain a phony self-image must have finally gotten to Daniel. I think he's simply a very unhealthy man, and I pray he stays out of my life.

Chapter Seven

Shortly after nine-thirty on Friday morning, CC arrived at the recycling center. Saralyn was making a fresh pot of coffee when Matt and Ben walked by the big office window. At first Saralyn had her back toward the window, so she didn't see them.

"So, girlfriend, is that the new manager out there walking with Ben? The one you hired to help out around here?" CC asked. "Do you know if he's married or not?"

"You know we can't ask questions like that during interviews," Saralyn answered casually, even though she had to admit having wondered the same thing. "But I don't think he is."

"So far, he has been an excellent employee and a great help for Ben. Coffee's ready. Let's go sit in the conference room, shall we?"

As Saralyn handed CC her cup of coffee, they walked into the nearby conference room.

"Matt has had some previous experience with the recycling business, you know, and with some of the computer software programs we use."

"Hmm, Matt is it?" CC teased. "You're already on such an informal first-name basis? Sounds like you might be a little impressed with the new guy. He is kinda cute, in a rugged sort of way."

"Come on, CC" Saralyn defended herself, smiling. "Besides, I'm probably too old for him, anyway. And I'm his boss. You know what a mess that could be."

Eventually, the tone of their conversation turned more serious. Saralyn's self-esteem had taken another beating.

"You know, I need to put this entire Daniel episode behind me. Sometimes I wonder, CC, maybe it's not so bad just being numb. I didn't have to feel anything. Daniel's words would not have been able to affect me like this."

"Listen to me, Saralyn. Good riddance! You are lucky to have seen the red flag warnings. Daniel is extremely obsessed with himself. A lot of women would have taken him back just to have a man around, even though he's verbally abusive. You don't need that! Thank God you had the discernment to end whatever it is you had going with him. He may not have told the truth about anything! Just what kind of work does he really do now? Some new biotech company? Remember, Daniel never even gave you a number to reach him during the day. Maybe he's not working at all!"

While pouring them both fresh cups of coffee, Saralyn changed the subject. "CC, I don't know what's going on lately. There are so many strange things happening around town. I told you Monday, when we talked on the phone, what happened at church Sunday. And who in the world was that woman watching everyone at the mall last week?"

Saralyn was hoping CC would understand. "I don't want people to think I'm paranoid or anything, but I'm really concerned that many of our friends and family are desensitized to unusual events—and that includes what's been happening around Oakbrook lately."

Saralyn's friend was understanding. "You don't have to convince me any. Wait until I tell you what's been happening at the children's center." CC had concerns of her own. "I'm really worried about the increase in abandoned babies. It's getting harder to find good foster care while these children are waiting for permanent placement.

"I think more babies are being abandoned because of all the drug abuse, and a lot of it is from antidepressants prescribed by doctors right in my building at the government clinic. Some call them 'mood altering' drugs, and others say they're 'mind altering.' You've heard of MADS?"

Saralyn nodded. "Just like Andrew was talking about. I forgot to mention, he ran in to Daniel recently. Andrew thought he looked pretty high on something."

CC continued, "It looks like the government will be taking over more of the everyday, routine activities at the center. They're even bringing in a civil service director from the government."

"Have you met this new director yet?" asked Saralyn.

"No, not yet, although there are already changes. I don't think she starts until next week."

"A *she*, hmm. Did I tell you that Daniel's sister Marcy has accepted a new government position?"

"No, you didn't mention it. I don't think the new director's name is Marcy, though. I'll have to check the memo when I get back to the office. Whatever her name is, she's instituted some ridiculous new and lengthy procedures. It'll create an overload of work for me and others." CC spoke with a sad expression, "You know, it's not going to be the same with all of the new rules and regulations. After I've worked so hard for some of these babies, I hate to see a bunch of new, lengthy procedures and burdensome, red tape paperwork interfering."

"Frustrating, isn't it?" Saralyn offered sympathetically. "We got away from those corporate, political, game-playing types, with their hidden agendas and their routine discrimination against honest people. Now it all seems to be catching up with us again."

Saralyn patted her friend's shoulder in an understanding gesture. Then she decided to ask CC about something more pleasant.

"So tell me, what's happening with Eddie?"

CC's expression brightened. She was proud of her only son; it hadn't been easy for him to get to where he was today.

"Eddie tells me they seem to be happy with his work out at the military base," CC said. "You know, we talk on the phone every few days or so. He gets along well with everyone he works with. The majority of them were all active-duty military at some time in their past. His new roommate in the apartment works at the base too. Eddie says that John—I think that's his name—used to be in the Navy. They carpool, but they actually work in different buildings and across base from each other."

"CC," Saralyn suddenly thought of an idea and decided to ask, "maybe you could check with Eddie to see if he has noticed anything strange going on out there. Specifically, could you ask him about those strange gray coats? When we were at the mall last week, was that the first time you had noticed anyone different?"

"No, now that we've talked about it, I did notice someone new at the Center a couple of weeks ago. I really didn't think anything about it at the time, because there are other divisions in our building. You know, maybe he did have a gray coat on, but I just figured he was a medical type. Most of the volunteer doctors and nurses do wear lab coats."

"I wish we had longer to visit," CC said, noting the time. "So, did Keri say anything to you about her seeing someone for depression?"

Saralyn hadn't heard. "She was a little quiet at last week's lunch, wasn't she? I wondered how she was doing, but I didn't want to pry unless she volunteered the info."

"Well, Keri mentioned to me that her medical insurance would cover most of the cost of a dozen visits or so to a therapist." Concerned and hopeful, CC continued, "I just hope she finds a good one—not someone who starts filling her head with garbage about how an individual doesn't have to be accountable for any of their actions."

"There are good Christian counselors out there who won't immediately put her on a lot of different drugs. Maybe we can find some referrals for her at church," Saralyn suggested, and then reminded herself out loud, "I have to make myself a note to give Keri a call later tonight. I know she can't really take phone calls at work during the day."

"She mentioned that one of her coworkers is really quite the hall monitor type," CC said, recalling one of her most recent conversations with Keri.

"Oh yes! We know the type, don't we?" Saralyn's memories were similar.

"Sounds like you haven't forgotten that one gal either—the one who would run and tell the boss if she thought any one of us had spent more than thirty seconds on a personal phone call."

"That's the one! Colorful personality."

"It's that type of coworker who begs to be told to get a life."

Just then, Ben came walking in with Matt right beside him. CC waved smiling, "Hey, Ben. How's that leg doing?"

"Hello, CC. Long time no see. Leg's coming along just fine."

Ben didn't like to talk about his leg much to anyone. Saralyn still suspected that the injury might not be healing as it should.

"And who's this? Someone new?" CC wanted to know.

Ben introduced Matt. "CC, this is Matthew Arboles. I'm letting him help out around here, since business has picked up so much."

"Well, nice to meet you, Mr. Arboles." Matt stepped forward to shake CC's hand.

"Please, call me Matt."

"So, Matt, are you married?"

Saralyn, eyes wide, couldn't believe what she'd just heard. Leave it to CC. She definitely was not shy.

Matt, smiling, indicated with a shrug that he wasn't. "No. No, I'm not married."

Ben held up a stack of papers in his hand. "Say, Saralyn, you wanted to go over this batch of invoices from yesterday at around ten-thirty. Is now a good time, or do you want us to come back a little later?"

"Oh my goodness! I can't believe how fast time flies by." CC realized she was running late. "I need to get back to the center. Nice meeting you, Matt. Bye, Ben. Hope to see you both soon."

She faced Saralyn and quickly added, "Walk me out to the parking lot real quick, will you?"

Ben and Matt said goodbye simultaneously and Saralyn started to escort CC outside when she turned and said, "Thanks for the reminder, Ben. I'll be right back. We'll go over those invoices then, OK? Just give me two minutes."

As Saralyn and CC rushed out toward CC's car, Saralyn quickly added, "I forgot to show you all the beautiful roses around the side of the building. Those bushes are blooming like crazy. I thought you might like to take some back to your office. Well, I'll bring you a bouquet next time I visit the center."

"OK, I'll hold you to it." Then, CC started to tease Saralyn again about Matt. "Well, your new manager does have a nice - smile. I even saw a little bit of gray in that thick, straggly hair. I personally, don't think he looks too young. He's probably just the right age for you—or me. Why don't you give *him* a bouquet of roses. See you later, girlfriend!"

Chapter Eight

At twelve-thirty, a couple of hours after CC had left, Saralyn went out to the lunch truck. She said hi to Ben on the way, and they chatted briefly about the shipment due in that afternoon. Saralyn purchased a soda from the drink machine, and it was then that her eyes met Matt's—just for an instant. Feeling vaguely uncomfortable, Saralyn had a hard time admitting to herself that she was attracted to him. She told herself that there could never be anything between them. He was probably too young and he was an employee. He was . . . *I don't need excuses,* she scolded herself, *there's nothing to worry or stress out about here.*

As she walked back to her office, she looked out toward the street. Just for a moment, Saralyn thought she saw Daniel's car sitting across the street and down a block. Later, when she got to her office, the car was gone.

Just before she walked through her door, Saralyn saw Matt again. He was standing outside toward the back of the loading dock near tall stacks of newspapers. It looked like some of the guys were good-naturedly making fun of him. One of them gave Matt a playful punch on the arm. Matt appeared to be joking right along with them.

Saralyn became extremely busy that afternoon. She was in and out of the files, on the phone, and working on the computer. Ben popped in to say goodnight about 4:30pm. Before she realized how much time had passed, it was 5:45.

Saralyn started to turn off the computer systems. Ben was responsible for securing the outside system and the big double doors. She had flipped off half of the switches when she heard a noise. She was startled to hear the door open, and then relieved to see Matt standing there.

"I thought you had gone home long ago. It's almost six," she said.

"I had some paperwork to finish up, and I wanted to make sure it was ready first thing Monday morning. I didn't mean to startle you." As Matt approached Saralyn, she felt a little uncomfortable.

She started to walk out the back door, then stopped for a minute to explain. "I just need to check all the other locks and windows for the weekend. It will just take a second."

"Well, I'll walk along with you for a few minutes, if you don't mind."

"No, of course not," she responded hesitantly and not altogether truthfully.

It took only moments until they made it around to the side of the building where Saralyn had planted roses and where the guys frequently took lunch breaks. Along with the rose garden, Ben and Saralyn had decided to put some benches in the shade, which provided employees with a place to sit outside when the weather was nice.

"How is everything working out for you here?" she inquired politely. "You know, during your first days on the job?"

"Well, thanks for asking. The job's going well."

Matt was facing her. Through his thin T-shirt, she noticed the movement of his chest with each breath he took. She wasn't completely certain about continuing her questions, but then she decided to ask, "Were the rest of the guys giving you a bad time today?"

"Oh, the little punching episode! No, that was nothing," Matt said, defending their playful activities. "The guys were teasing me about my last name. You know, my Spanish is not as good as it used to be." He explained further, "The other fellows thought I might not even know what *Arboles* translates to. I played along with them for a while and said it means 'big, strong white man.'"

Saralyn laughed along with Matt's chuckle.

"It means *trees*, right?" She offered a guess.

"Right."

"So, your Spanish is basically good enough to understand the guys when they talk among themselves?" she asked.

"Well, sometimes. When there are more than two or three of the guys speaking fast together, I get lost. I should probably brush up some; it never hurts to be bilingual. Although Ben tells me that most of the recycling employees speak pretty good English too."

Looking at and pointing toward the roses, Matt asked with a smile, "Speaking of brushing up on our Spanish, how do you say 'beautiful roses'?"

"Wait, I know this." Saralyn thought for a moment. "Oh, it's not *las flores*, is it? I know that means 'the flowers.' Give me a minute," she said smiling, "I used to know this. Is it something like *rosa*? *Las rosas bellas*?"

"Well, I'm impressed," Matt offered graciously.

"Thank you, thank you," Saralyn gave a mock curtsy. "I had better get going. My daughter Breanne will be expecting something for dinner. Hopefully, she hasn't eaten a ton of junk food already." Saralyn continued hesitantly, and with caution, "Do you have any children?"

"Yes, actually I do, one son. His name is Thomas. His mother left and divorced me some years ago. She took him with her back to Washington, D.C., for some . . . job opportunities. Unfortunately, I don't get to see him very often. I flew back for a visit last year. Things were uncomfortable a lot of the time, but it was so good to see him."

Saralyn was grateful for Matt's honesty.

It sounded as if talking about his son was painful for him. What was she feeling right now? Maybe sympathy. His nearness was becoming a little unnerving.

She was beginning to feel kind of clumsy. Was it chemistry, this reaction she was having to his closeness?

Matt could sense that she was going to leave any second, so he knew that he needed to continue quickly. "Well anyway, Saralyn, I just wanted to say I noticed the framed scripture verse at your desk."

"Yes." Saralyn had no clue what he might say next. Was he going to complain about having any displays of religion in the workplace?

Matt continued, "I left seminary when my wife left me."

"Really! I don't mean to act so surprised. It's just, I would never have guessed." Saralyn was looking into his eyes shyly. She was interested in all that he was saying.

He briefly looked away, then returned her gaze warmly. "I was angry at the turn of events in my life. I missed my son from the very moment he left. Now I'm grateful to be back on track. I probably won't return to seminary, but I'm at peace with the decision."

"Well, thank God. I'm definitely glad to hear you're back on track." Saralyn replied. Once again, she was genuinely surprised at his news. *Who would have guessed? That just goes to show, you really can't judge a book by its cover.* I'm glad I've kept that scripture plaque out in plain sight for all to see.

"I'd really better get going now. I'm glad to hear that everything is working out here on the job. Ben tells me you've stepped right in and have learned some of the newer computer software systems quickly. Good work."

Saralyn had learned that it was important to offer supportive words of acknowledgement and appreciation to individual employees who deserved praise. She understood this completely, especially, since she and many of her coworkers and friends had not received encouragement while working in the corporate environment. She shouldn't feel any different offering it to Matt. But she did.

"Thank you, Saralyn, for this job opportunity. My motto is 'Any job worth doing is worth doing well.' I think the saying goes something like that."

They both laughed, "Goodnight."

He gave her a sort of half-salute wave. She smiled back at him and made a similar gesture. "Have a good weekend, Matt. We'll talk more next week."

And they did talk more. The next week, the week after that, and through the following months.

Chapter Nine

Meanwhile, that same Friday was the third day of school for Breanne. One of her new friends, Dawn, started public school for the first time, since she could not continue her home schooling. Dawn's mother tried to renew her home-teaching license several times but had not been successful. The license had become ridiculously expensive, which made getting it impossible for most parents.

The government created the difficult, red tape situation. Now there was virtually no home schooling being allowed anywhere.

Breanne originally introduced herself to Dawn the previous day, since they had a couple of classes together. Dawn looked to Breanne like she was a bit lost and perhaps scared in her new environment.

Dawn was a pretty teenager with dark brown hair and light blue eyes. She wore minimal to no make-up and had high cheek bones, making her look as if she could be part Native American.

Dawn was grateful for Breanne's kindness. She was quite nervous and was struggling to get used to public school. After being taught at home all these years, this new experience proved to be intimidating.

As a couple of Breanne's friends from the previous year met up at the lunch benches, Breanne introduced them to Dawn.

"Becca and Nicky, this is Dawn."

"Hey, Dawn, I think I saw you in first-period history. Mr. Darian seems OK so far, but I've heard his tests might be hard," Nicky offered.

"Yes," Dawn answered, "I have history first period. Maybe we could get each other's telephone numbers, just in case we forget a homework assignment or something."

The other three girls exchanged an is-she-for-real look. Then Dawn tried to explain. "My mother has drilled into me that it will be extremely important to exchange numbers with at least one student in each of my classes."

"Sure, why not? Breanne, is this where you and Becca are going to be eating lunch everyday?" asked Nicky.

"Yeah, usually. I think so," said Breanne.

"Probably. I guess so," added Becca.

Breanne didn't mind bringing her lunch almost every day, because it gave her a little extra time to visit with friends. When she didn't have to stand in long lunch lines at the cafeteria, there was more time to get homework done early too.

Today, there was going to be a special assembly. Most of the kids were talking about it. The majority of them figured that it was going to be some routine, beginning-of-the-year announcements and a pep rally. Breanne figured that the school administration would probably be reminding everyone about the lame, new dress-code policies.

Breanne, Dawn, Becca, and Nicky started to walk toward the gym together after finishing their lunches.

"Let's sit kinda close to the main door so it doesn't take us forever to get out. OK guys?" requested Becca.

"Maybe we'll find out about those new, bigger lockers that no one seems to be assigned to yet," Nicky wondered out loud.

"Hey, did you see what's his name in science?"

Becca explained to Dawn, "Breanne had a crush on him last year."

"Hardly! What are you talking about Becca?" Breanne said defensively. "You're the one who thought he was so cute!"

The girls continued to tease each other about boys and about who liked whom, until they reach the gym.

The gym was a madhouse. Teenagers were everywhere, yelling to get some friend's attention.

It was 12:45 P.M., time for the assembly to officially start. The assistant principal, Mrs. Sterling, walked up to the platform.

"OK, ladies and gentlemen, everyone find a seat. It's important to stay on schedule here. You don't want to be late for the rest of your classes, now do you?"

Some moans, some laughs from the audience of high schoolers, as everyone found his or her seat.

Mrs. Sterling continued, "Let me start by welcoming you back to school. This promises to be a great year. Also, let me take this opportunity to officially welcome all of our new students to Oakbrook High School. Wherever you come to us from, we hope you will find your experiences here at Oakbrook to be good ones."

Breanne, Nicky, and Becca all looked to Dawn, rolling their eyes upward with smiles and nods.

"Yep, this sounds like the same speech as last year," whispered Nicky.

Nancy Sterling was ready for retirement. She had worked for the school district for thirty years now and was highly educated. There were a lot of changes coming up—changes she wasn't too thrilled about. However, she mostly kept quiet now concerning situations she felt may be objectionable. She did not want to jeopardize her tenure when she was so near to retirement. The school board suggested that things wouldn't go well for anyone who complained about upcoming changes. One more year—that was all she needed before retiring. One more school year.

"For those who don't know me, my name is Mrs. Sterling. I am the assistant principal here at Oakbrook. I want to remind everyone to read over your dress-code handouts you were all given in first period. The administration will begin to write up those not following these guidelines, and we will issue suspension warnings starting next week.

"You'll notice our cafeteria has been remodeled somewhat, and you can pick up new menus from the cashier window. Now, let me introduce to you our principal, Mr. Murphy, who has some exciting news."

Mr. Murphy stood up to walk toward the microphone. He was a tall man with an authoritative voice, but he also had a friendly and approachable manner. He was around fifty years old and had thick gray hair. In years past, he had sometimes substituted for the basketball coach when needed.

"We have a great opportunity to participate in some ground-breaking technology." Mr. Murphy believed in getting right to the point. "Starting next Monday, every student will have the option to sign up for one of the new, larger, remodeled lockers. If you choose to volunteer for the new lockers, you will also have much easier access to the school computers."

By now, all of the students sitting in the gym were looking at each other with questioning expressions on their faces and whispering, "What in the world is he talking about?"

The principal continued, "I would now like to introduce to you Mr. Sierra. He will explain to you about the demonstration."

Mr. Sierra stood and walked toward the microphone. In front of him, he pushed a square table that was like a cart on wheels. On top of the table sat one of the new lockers. As Mr. Sierra raised his hand and began to speak, the noise level, which consisted of many voices, became subdued.

"Most of you probably can't see this. There is a very tiny bump on the top of my left hand, right here." He pointed to it with his right index finger. "It is just under the skin between my left thumb and index finger. It's about the size of a dime, only it's shape is square. On this implanted chip is my name, date of birth, and social security number. That's all!" Mr. Sierra was animated, in an attempt to infect the students with his excitement.

"And believe me, ladies and gentlemen, this is amazing, cutting-edge technology. Let me demonstrate, along with Mr. Murphy, just exactly how it all works." Mr. Murphy turned the locker toward Mr. Sierra while closing the door and making sure it was locked. Mr. Sierra, then enthusiastically instructed his audience, "I want you all to watch carefully."

The students had become very quiet. They did listen and watch with anticipation.

"All you need to do is gently slide the back of your hand across this square, black panel and there you go!" The locker silently popped open. "No kicking or banging because the locker is stuck and won't open. No forgetting your locker number and being stuck with heavy books all day long."

In the crowd behind and around Breanne, there were several murmurs of "awesome," "wow" and other voices whispering, "You've got to be kidding me." Breanne and her friends were speechless.

"Implanting this small chip is completely pain free and simple—a very minor procedure," Mr. Sierra explained. "The chip is manufactured locally, and it is made with biotechnologically developed materials that are compatible with everyone's skin and blood type. The chip won't hurt; it doesn't itch, either. I have had mine for approximately six months now, and most of the time I don't even remember it's there. Well, let me turn things back over to your principal, Mr. Murphy. I hope each and every one of you will have the opportunity, at some point in the near future, to take advantage of this exciting new technology."

Mr. Murphy returned to the microphone and held up a stack of papers. "For anyone wanting to apply to be one of the first to participate, here are the forms you need to fill out." Then the principal added, "This is something that doesn't even require a parent's signature. You can just complete the form and turn it in to your last-period teacher before leaving school."

Breanne and her friends started to leave the gym. They were, at first, unsure of all they had just heard.

Becca asked, "What do you guys think?"

"Maybe, its not such a bad thing. Just think, we could be one of the first," said Nicky. "I'll go pick up an application for each of us."

Later that evening, Breanne told her mother about what happened at school. Saralyn was shocked, but tried to restrain her initial angry reaction. She wanted to know if Mr. Sierra appeared to be a government representative.

"Was he wearing a gray lab coat?" she asked Breanne.

"What are you asking that for, Mom? Who cares, and what difference does it make?"

Breanne told her mom there had been no gray lab coat. However, after thinking back to the assembly, she remembered he had been wearing some kind of lab coat. But she didn't want to mention it to her mom and, instead, told Saralyn that she worried too much.

"Nicky and the other kids are going to do it! You should be grateful I even mentioned this to you. Most of the kids aren't going to say a word to their parents," Breanne said, reminding her mom that students didn't need parental permission to sign up for the implant. "At least the school treated us like adults this morning. We don't need anyone's permission to sign up for one of the new lockers if we want to."

Saralyn prayed silently that God would provide her with the appropriate words. She knew it would be crucial to ensure that Breanne not turn in those forms to become a volunteer.

"Yes, Breanne. Thank you for sharing this news with me. Please, please, please, don't follow the crowd on this one. Don't even think about it, OK, honey? Just imagine. The school administration would be able to know where you are at all times. They will probably have some kind of location tracking devices included on those implanted chips."

"Don't be ridiculous, Mom. It's just for opening our lockers and signing on to the computers. You sound so paranoid."

Thankfully, Breanne had her own doubts. Eventually, she realized that her mom might be right.

After Breanne had gone to bed that evening, Saralyn gave CC a telephone call.

"Slow down a bit. You're talking too fast, and speak louder!" CC scolded. What did you say about Breanne?"

"I said that her school had an all-student assembly today. The principal and a guest speaker gave a demonstration for some kind of a computer chip implanted just below the skin on the back of the hand."

"Implanted?"

"Yes, implanted! Can you believe this? It's all voluntary, they say, for now. But they were encouraging the kids to take advantage of this 'great opportunity,' and the sooner the better. And get this, CC: The kids were told they don't even need parental approval."

"Dear Lord!" CC declared. "I guess I shouldn't be so surprised. After all, nature organizations have been tracking animals for years now with some type of little implanted devices. I saw this wildlife program not too long ago about these implants in endangered species. The next step is children, of course."

"Breanne heard some of the teachers talking," Saralyn continued, wanting to fill in more details. "The high school has been approached with the implant program first. This way the older kids might have more of a big sister/big brother influence on the younger children. Eventually, the implants will be presented to all the elementary grades as well."

"What did you say to her?" CC asked.

"I've asked Breanne not to, of course. I tried to explain to her that with this implant, the school could probably keep track of her every move. I'm hopeful that will convince her for now." Then Saralyn asked her friend, "CC, do you remember I told you Daniel had recently changed jobs—that he's now working for some small, local, biotech company. Maybe, he's working at the same place that manufactures these implants. I think I might call the pastor of my church tomorrow. Possibly he has heard about all this and has further insight. I should also ask him if he noticed that man visiting church last week. I think he might be from the government too."

"Speaking of government, let me tell you about my conversation with Eddie Jr. earlier this evening."

"What did he have to say?" Saralyn eagerly inquired.

"Eddie tells me that he has, in fact, seen a group of new personnel out at the base. And, get this, he thought they were medical types or something because they were all wearing those gray lab coats."

"Oh no, CC! What's going on here?"

"Wait, it gets even better." CC told Saralyn more of the conversation she'd had with her son. "Eddie said he walked right by some guy wearing the knee-length jacket. He was close enough to read his nametag. Are you sitting down?"

"Yes, I am now. Go on," Saralyn replied in a hushed tone.

"His nametag said WORLD ORDER ORGANIZATION. The guys out at the base have even started calling them the WOOS. These representatives don't mingle with the rest of the military troops or with civilian personnel. All of the World Order people keep pretty much to themselves!"

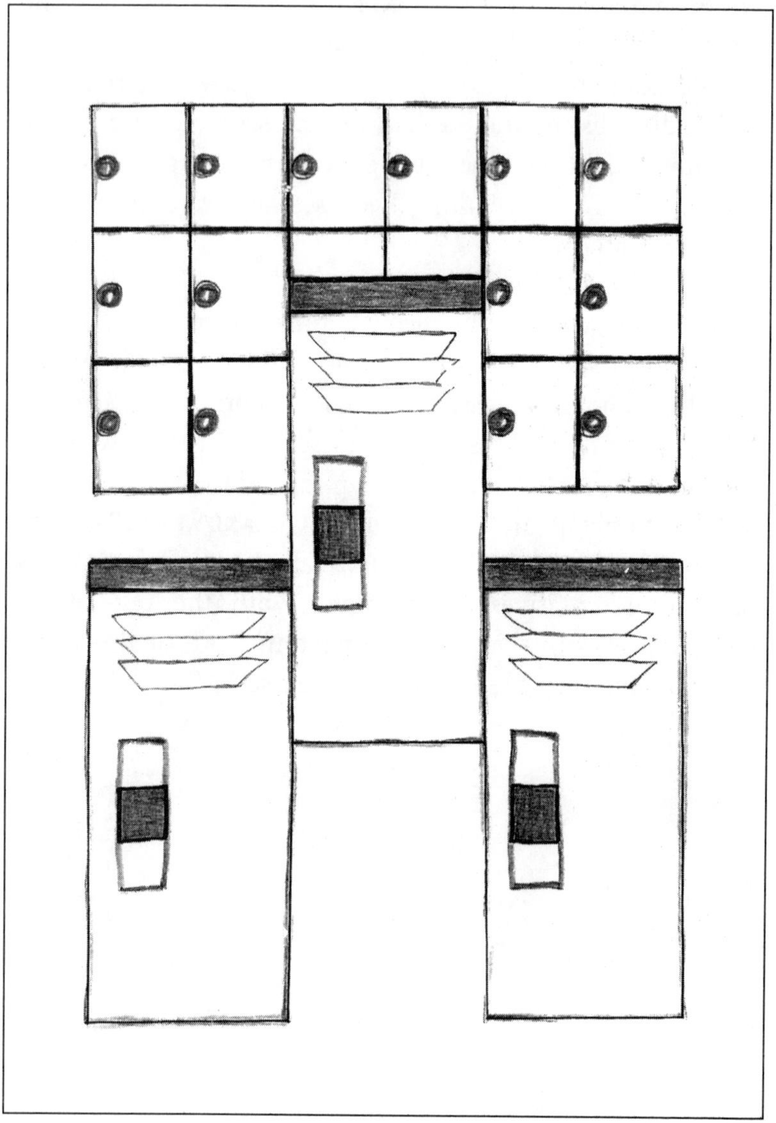

Part Two

Christmas Season 1999

Chapter Ten

It became widely known that the strangers in gray lab coats, who were popping up all over the place, were representatives of the growing one-world-order organization. Most everyone referred to them as WOOS. Approximately three-and-a-half months—September, October, November, and part of December—had passed without any further big surprises.

The weather was still warm, though it rained occasionally, similar to a tropical climate. Many people went about their business, wearing light, summer clothing—unusual even for California.

Matt and the other guys at the recycling center still performed some of the heavy lifting work without wearing their shirts.

Fire season had still not ended in some parts of the United States. Across the country, areas that normally cooled down significantly in winter had not done so. Weather patterns were mixed up all over the world.

All of Matt's fellow employees learned that his Hispanic father had never gotten around to becoming a citizen and had disappeared approximately one year ago. Matt hadn't heard from him since.

There had been scattered reports from other individuals that their family members or loved ones had mysteriously disappeared. The majority of incidents were not taken seriously by authorities, so the disappearances were not investigated. None of the missing persons were American citizens.

Matt and Saralyn continued to cultivate a friendship. They had become closer. She remained concerned, however, about their roles in the workplace. She did realize that it was often hard for a lot of men not to feel emasculated when women were in charge. It didn't seem to bother Matt, though. She also worried that, because of her age, he might not be seriously interested in anything more than friendship, although she discovered he was thirty-nine years old, which made him only six years younger.

Saralyn definitely felt something more than friendship toward Matt. She wasn't quite sure what, if anything, to do about it. She was surprised by the intensity of her feelings, since she believed those deeper emotions were forever numbed by earlier disastrous relationships. Matt and Saralyn had become accustomed to sharing long talks after work. She was more comfortable around him now, and very much looked forward to the end of their work day.

Matt and Ben had become better friends as well. They usually spoke with each other away from the rest of the guys. Matt believed Ben's heart had been prepared by God and that he was ready to learn more about salvation. An argument Ben made against Christianity had to do with negative and derogatory comments about fundamentalist

Christians made by other individuals who also called themselves Christian.

Matt explained that being fundamentalist actually referred to people who did not just choose to believe only the fragmented parts of the Bible that fit in with their lifestyle.

Ben's leg never healed properly, and he continued to walk with a slight limp. He would not return to any of the medical facilities to receive further treatment for fear he would be forced into retirement by authorities.

Saralyn discovered the reason for Ben's concerns. One of Ben's buddies, Joe, had hurt his back. He was in his late fifties, his back was slowly getting better, and he felt he was still capable of performing his teaching duties. Joe had taught college classes for ten years. After going to his doctor for a routine follow-up exam, Joe was given a notice of mandatory retirement. He tried to fight it, arguing he was confident his back was healing. It didn't matter. Joe had to make arrangements to leave his job within thirty days.

Oakbrook High School refurbished more of the old, small lockers into the newer, bigger, fancier ones that required the implanted chip to open them. So far, fifty percent of the high-school students had been given the opportunity to use one of the lockers.

Among Breanne's closest friends, Becca and Nicky had undergone the minor procedure to implant the identity chip. Only Dawn and Breanne continued to hold out, choosing not to turn in the required applications.

There were numerous preparations being made for turn-of-the-century New Year's Eve parties and celebrations. In the upcoming weeks, there would be activities all over the world.

Some of the New Year's Eve festivities were expected to last for days. Marissa, along with many of her friends and acquaintances at the shopping mall, where most of them worked, were planning to throw one big party of their own.

Pastor Dave continued to teach from the Book of John during the last several months. He explained that while Jesus performed many miracles during his ministry and had been a charismatic teacher, it was the fact that He had been crucified, suffered, died on the cross, and then ascended to heaven, that provided all believers with everlasting life. No matter how good an individual tried to be, he or she could never be good enough to earn salvation. No matter how many good deeds or rules one person followed, heaven cannot be entered by human effort.

Jesus was the only son of God. He is God, Lord, and Savior. There is no other way to make it to heaven except for through belief in Him. Pastor Dave finished his teaching from John's gospel before Christmas. He ended with the seven "I am" statements Jesus made about Himself: the Bread of Life; the Light of the World; the Door of the Sheep; the Good Shepherd; the Resurrection and the Life; the True Vine; the Way, the Truth, and the Life.

Saralyn found comfort in Jesus' promises. She thought of God sometimes in terms of a big quilt. She was wrapped up in His protective comforting love, kept warm and safe. No other man was around.

Saralyn had not heard anything further from Daniel. Thank God. Unfortunately, she had heard less and less from Andrew as well. He was in her thoughts and prayers daily. Saralyn also continued to pray for Marissa, who made the choice to stay away from weekly church services. She was looking forward to another opportune time to remind her oldest daughter about the story in the Bible of the ten virgins.

Dear Lord, please bless us all with wisdom and discernment.

Chapter Eleven

The malls were decorated for the Christmas season . . . sort of. There were holiday displays throughout most of the aisle areas. Saralyn walked slowly by the festive holiday decorations. In many stores, religious Christmas decorations, gifts, and cards had been pushed behind the numerous suggestions for new-millennium parties. "Jingle Bells" and "Santa Claus is Coming to Town" music played loudly throughout the mall.

In years past, Saralyn mused to herself, *many Christians mentioned that merchants and their paying customers had all but forgotten the true meaning of Christmas.*

This year, however, that observation appeared particularly true. The real reason for this season had been put on the back shelves in many stores, to make room for New Year's Eve streamers and party hats.

Today, Saralyn was shopping for one more gift. She needed to find this one, last, special present before she attended the afternoon brunch Christmas party with CC, Wendy, Deborah, and Keri.

Over the years, they had all discovered what special gifts were just right for each other. For instance, Deborah collected angels and enjoyed African art; CC loved unique picture frames and candles; Keri appreciated new clothes or real perfume, because she normally spent the clothing budget on her children and routinely purchased imitation brands of colognes for herself; and Wendy collected Native American art, especially eagles.

Saturdays between Thanksgiving and Christmas were typically busy, and this morning was no exception. Saralyn decided to sit down for a few moments and take a break at one of the three coffee shops in the mall. While ordering her coffee drink, she was recognized and then approached by an old work acquaintance.

"Hey, Saralyn, where in the world have you been hiding?"

"Oh, hi, Jessica."

Saralyn was friendly. However, she was hopeful Jessica would not stay and chat.

"Wow, how have you been? It's been so long since I've seen you around. Did you really go and open some kind of recycling center?"

Jessica continued to talk as she spotted a small table near the corner. Then she picked up both of their coffees and carried them over to the table and sat down.

Saralyn's first instinct was to run the other direction, but she was really looking forward to that cup of coffee.

"Of all the businesses you could have opened, I simply can't believe you actually did that. Is business OK? You're probably not doing very well, huh, what with all the new regulations and such?"

"Well, actually Jessica, all those new regulations have significantly increased business."

"Oh, really." Jessica tried again, "Well, old friend, I still don't see any wedding ring on that finger of yours. What's up, Saralyn? Still not remarried?"

Even though Jessica was trying unsuccessfully to sound sympathetic, Saralyn also realized that she was just baiting her.

"I'm actually dating two different men. They're both really great. I just can't choose." Saralyn shrugged her shoulders and smiled, but silently she scolded herself because what she had just said was not completely true. *I shouldn't let her bother me like this.* For some reason, Saralyn just couldn't resist.

Sadly, Jessica hadn't changed any. She was the infamous hall monitor when CC, Deborah, Keri, Wendy, and Saralyn all worked together in the same corporate department. Jessica had always been digging for gossip, and if she didn't find anything interesting enough, unfortunately she would ultimately make some up. She was also very paranoid about what others might be saying about her. So, in her obsessive paranoia, whatever stories she made up generally made others look bad. Her defense was always a strong, if completely misguided, offense.

Jessica also had an uncanny ability of taking credit for special projects that others around her worked hard on. It was frustrating, that for some unknown reason, management always seemed to believe her stories. The majority of Saralyn's coworkers used to joke among themselves that Jessica must have compromising pictures on one of their department's senior managers. Management was truly blind to Jessica's manipulative behavior, and a lot of employees, including Saralyn, had to suffer the consequences.

"So, Jessica, what are you up to?" Saralyn asked in an attempt to take the spotlight off herself, as she took a sip of coffee.

"Oh, the usual. I've recently been promoted, you know. My work is always better quality than most. Department management recognizes the excellence of my job performance. A lot of the women I work with now don't like me, but they are just jealous, of course."

"Of course."

Jessica had a certain way of sticking out her chest whenever she boasted about herself or was trying to make an impression.

"I'm not bragging, you know, but my husband has recently received a great promotion too. We're thinking about looking for a new, bigger house."

"You don't say." *Sometimes lots of great things happen to people like Jessica. Well, it's just material stuff,* Saralyn consoled herself.

"Last night my husband brought me the most beautiful display of flowers you have ever seen."

I have just about heard enough! Saralyn did not think she could bear to listen to much more, but she said, "Really!"

"Yes, they're absolutely gorgeous. I'm thinking about taking half of the flowers in to work Monday. Oh, by the way, speaking of work, I hear Keri is not doing so well. She's missed a lot of work lately, and there've been rumors that she'll probably end up with very negative remarks on her yearly review."

How did Jessica discover that sensitive information, especially concerning someone else's personnel review—someone who worked not only in another department but in another building altogether?

"Keri has always been a real sweetheart. Maybe, she's just going through some rough times," Saralyn defended her old coworker friend. Then, she remarked, "Well, Jessica, I really do have some shopping to finish up."

Saralyn tipped her cup to finish the last drops of coffee and stood to leave. "Take care, Jessica, and Merry Christmas."

"You, too, Saralyn. Good to see you. Merry Xmas."

Saralyn shook her head ever so slightly as she walked away to finish up her shopping. *Why must people insist on taking the Christ out of Christmas?*

Saralyn had yet to find just the right gift for Wendy. In the past, the women had drawn names and then had spent an agreed-upon amount on that one gift. Usually, the limit was approximately twenty to twenty-five dollars. However, they all usually brought smaller gifts for each name they hadn't drawn. Plus, every year Saralyn exchanged gifts with CC.

This Saturday morning, Saralyn was thinking about looking in the candle store for Wendy's present. *Most everyone loves some sort of candle,* she reminded herself, and this year Saralyn had drawn Wendy's name. Maybe some type of candle with a Native American theme.

She had already spent many evenings and weekends making gifts out of recycled materials. Last year Saralyn made Christmas placemats for CC, Deborah, Keri, and Wendy, as well as for other friends and neighbors.

It was Saralyn's mother who taught her how to make the placemats from recycled Christmas cards. It was time-consuming, but gave Saralyn a feeling of creativity. Each placemat required approximately eighteen Christmas cards, each of which had to be cut into a circle. Every mat needed a backing of decorative self-adhesive shelf paper and a top covering made of clear self-sticking paper.

This year Saralyn had decided to make little drum Christmas-tree ornaments that she would include with sheet music from "The Little Drummer Boy." The drums were made of recycled plastic bottle caps from milk and juice containers. Each drum also required little bits of plastic, canvas, some yarn, and approximately ten gold, red, or silver beads.

As Saralyn finished up her last-minute shopping at the Oakbrook Mall, she looked forward to seeing everyone later that day at their Christmas brunch.

Chapter Twelve

"Where is Wendy?" asked Deborah.

Once again, Wendy had yet to make her late arrival. The friends, who had gathered for their annual potluck brunch, were all supposed to have met at two-thirty this Saturday afternoon. It was now three o'clock.

"Maybe we could relax for a few minutes and enjoy some sparkling apple cider. Or would anyone like something stronger? I have several different wines here," offered CC.

The brunch this year was at CC's home. She lived in an average-sized condominium—just right for one. She also possessed a definite talent for interior decorating. The condo included a comfortably large family room where CC normally set up her Christmas tree. This year was no exception. Her tree was beautiful! It wasn't really tall, or big, or wide, but she had decorated it with care and a certain flair.

CC's condo was about fifteen to seventeen miles from Saralyn's house on the other side of Oakbrook. CC often reminded the group how much she loved her two-bedroom, one-bath home, mainly because there was less space to clean.

Today, there were several scented Christmas candles burning in the bathroom. And from the kitchen came the smell of flavored coffee brewing along with the different foods each of the women had brought to share. Saralyn had brought one of her favorite dishes, and they were all looking forward to tasting the tempting foods.

Just as CC was uncorking a bottle of wine, there was a knock at the door.

Keri got up to answer it.

"Hello, everybody. Merry merry Christmas!"

"Come on in, Wendy. We've already eaten, but I think we managed to save at least one glass of wine," teased Deborah.

Wendy looked surprised. "What? I'm not that late, am I?"

As the others smiled, made eye contact with each other, and enjoyed the humor, Saralyn let Wendy in on the joke. "Just kidding. I think some of the food dishes are still warming in the oven. What did you bring?"

As they all settled in, visited with each other, and enjoyed the food, time went by quickly.

CC shared with everyone that her son was doing well. He had met a girl, and it seemed to be getting serious. "In fact, they're in my back bedroom right now, watching TV. I think they popped in with hopes that there would be leftovers."

Their hostess also discussed her concerns over the increased number of infants and children that were being-processed through the placement center. It was hard to look at their fearful faces all year. It was especially tough at this time of year. The foster family programs were in desperate need of volunteers. On a more positive note, she said that during the holidays church groups usually made an extra effort at gift giving and at baking Christmas cookies for the children. Some of the older children were visibly touched. However, it was often harder to cope when visits were over and the groups had to leave. Then the children were left lonely.

Keri was quiet, but she seemed more relaxed today than she had been during their last lunch together. She spoke about her own children and how the job wasn't bothering her as much as it used to.

Deborah spoke about the upcoming Christmas program at their church. Her husband was assisting in the direction of this year's play. She invited the group to attend.

Wendy was a little hesitant at first to volunteer information. This was out of character for her. Eventually, she shared the details about her current boyfriend. Wendy reminded everyone that she attempted to set up Saralyn with this great guy. However, now Wendy was dating him, and according to her, he was just the best person to come along in her life in a very long time.

Soon, brunch was over and it was time to open gifts.

CC had drawn Keri's name this year. As Keri slowly opened her package the others watched. Inside, was a beautiful green sweater made from very soft material. The gift was perfect for Keri. She always looked good in green.

"Thank you, CC. What a beautiful sweater!"

"Hold it up, Keri. Let's get a better look," requested Saralyn.

CC also distributed to Saralyn, Wendy, and Deborah some lovely Christmas-tree angels crafted from lace.

"OK, now my turn to hand out gifts," Keri decided to pass out her own.

To Wendy, CC, and Saralyn, she gave reindeer that had been uniquely handmade from recycled Popsicle sticks. Their cute faces were peeking up from Christmas tins full of candy canes. The reindeer had big, red, cotton-ball noses and green antlers.

"Oh, Keri. How darling these are," CC exclaimed sincerely.

"They really are," voiced both Wendy and Saralyn.

"Thanks, guys. The kids made them years ago in Sunday school, and I had kept the pattern. So this year, I came across the pattern again and couldn't resist."

Then to Deborah she handed a larger gift. Deborah turned toward Keri, genuinely thankful, "Keri, this is wonderful. Look everyone." Deborah held up a beautiful, hand-painted, leopard print on black material.

"Wherever did you find this?"

"At our company's Christmas boutique a few weeks ago." Then Keri was apologetic. "I'm sorry that it's not framed or anything. But maybe you'll be able to mat and frame it however you want."

"Oh, don't be ridiculous. It really doesn't matter whether it's framed or not. I love this—the colors, everything." Deborah gently placed the gift back in its box.

Wendy had drawn CC's name this year. She presented her with a large, flat, silver box that had a big, gold, metallic bow on top.

As CC tried to guess what was inside, Deborah coaxed, "All right already. Just open it, would you!"

Inside, was an oval wooden plaque with what appeared to be a picture of an open Bible engraved on the wood. On the plaque, in black, printed letters, was the story of Jesus' birth, through the words of the song "Away in a Manger."

"Wendy, this is truly unique . . . and beautiful. Thank you very much. I just love this, and I know the perfect place where I can display it."

For Keri, Deborah, and Saralyn, Wendy gave some fragrant hand lotions and small, thin bookmarks. The bookmarks also had Bible verses quoted on them.

"Thank you, Wendy. These are great. I love the smell of this lotion too." Deborah thanked her, as she twisted off the cap to her lotion and squeezed some out onto her hand.

"Did you get these from Lotions 'n' Lipsticks?" asked Saralyn.

"Yes, and I swore Marissa to secrecy, since she was working the day I purchased these and helped out with the selections. She promised she wouldn't tell."

"Well, she didn't."

CC asked Wendy, "Did you get the plaque from the Oakbrook Bible-and-Book store? This wood carving is gorgeous."

"No, I actually found it out of town. I'm so glad you like it."

"OK, Wendy. Your turn. Here you go, and handle with care. This is breakable." Saralyn handed Wendy a large, red, plastic bag that was tied at the top with lots of gold and silver ribbons.

Wendy gently untied the ribbons to unveil what was inside. She slowly lifted out of the bag, a one-and-a-half-foot candle carved into an American bald eagle. It's head was white, and the brown wings of the eagle were spread open as if in flight.

"Thank you very much, Saralyn. I truly love this."

"You're welcome. And now, here are some small goodies for the rest of you." Saralyn passed around the little drums she'd made, along with the sheet music to "The Little Drummer Boy."

"Well last, but not least." Deborah reached over and handed Saralyn her present in beautiful, gold wrapping paper with a red, velvet ribbon and bow.

"This is too pretty to open!" Saralyn exclaimed.

Inside, under the matching gold and white tissue paper was a large, picture book all about roses.

"This is perfect! Deborah, thank you!"

"Well, you mentioned your rosebushes the last time we all had lunch, and I came across this. There is a little something else in there. Did you miss it?"

As Saralyn felt around inside the box, in one of the corners she found a miniature bottle of pure rose perfume.

"This smells intoxicating. Thanks again, Deborah. I know I'll be enjoying both." Saralyn passed the rose perfume around for everyone to smell.

"And, for the rest of you guys, here you go." Deborah distributed stained glass candle holders, along with small candles to go inside.

"Thank you, very much, Deborah. Did you make these?" asked Keri.

"No, but aren't they just so pretty? I fell in love with them. Found them at the import store just outside of town."

"OK, now. Who all brought cameras? We must take some pictures. This is truly a festive Kodak moment," Saralyn said. Then she added, "Here's mine."

"Who's going to take the pictures?" Wendy asked.

"Let me go find my camera and ask Eddie and his girlfriend to do it. That way we all can be included," offered CC.

Then, she headed down the hall and knocked on the back bedroom door. Seconds later, CC reappeared with her two guests following close behind.

"Everyone, most of you have met Eddie Jr. This is his friend April."

"Hey, Eddie, good to see you again. It's been a long time, hasn't it? Merry Christmas. Nice to meet you, April." Wendy, Saralyn, Deborah, and Keri were all speaking at once.

"Did you hungry ladies save any food for us?" Eddie asked.

"There's plenty in there. But first you'll need to take some pictures of the group." His mom looked at him and asked, "OK? Please?"

"Sure, where are the cameras? Everyone say 'cheese.'"

"Wait, wait!" CC pleaded. "Let's all get together over here on the couch. Hang on just a second. Be patient."

"He must be hungry. We'd better not keep them waiting too long."

Saralyn suggested that two of the ladies sit on the small couch and three stand evenly centered behind them.

"Take a few shots, would you, Eddie? We want to make sure at least one of them turns out," Deborah recommended.

"I'd like copies." Wendy and Keri requested at the same time.

As the group finished their desserts, coffee, and wine, CC turned on some more Christmas music and performed a little dance on her way back to her seat.

"You go, girl. Let's see some of those moves." Deborah encouraged her.

"Well, I don't usually dance to 'Deck the Halls.' What does one do for 'fa-la-la-la-la'?" Then she pointed toward her son, "Look how easy it is to embarrass your children."

Eddie was visibly embarrassed, although in a good-natured way. He smiled, hanging his head down while he and April moved toward the kitchen to check out the leftovers.

Once CC had settled back into her comfortable chair, the music playing in the background, they had an opportunity to visit for a little while longer.

"I almost forgot to tell you all who I ran into at the mall this morning." Saralyn hesitated briefly, as she looked at the questioning anticipation in her friends faces. "It was Jessica, and she called me 'old friend.'" Saralyn recounted the details of her coffee café encounter.

Everyone offered various expressions of sympathy.

Keri reminded the group, "Jessica still works for the same department where we all worked together years ago. She's been promoted several times."

"Yes, she told me about her most recent promotion. Still, I can't help but almost feel sorry for her. She seemed so desperate to make an impression, regardless if it was true or not."

"I wonder if she still washes her face every night. In order to remove her make-up, just to reapply it all over again. Do you all remember?" Deborah asked. "She would go through the ritual so her husband would wake up to her all made up?"

"Yeah, I remember hearing that," Wendy said. "Well, you know what I always say."

"What's that, Wendy?" CC wondered.

"Don't criticize thy neighbor, until you have walked a mile in his or her moccasins."

"Well! Thank you very much, Wendy, for those native words of wisdom!" Deborah laughed, and then she added more seriously, "You're right, you know. Hard to say what's really going on in Jessica's life."

"You know, working in that department was one of the most awful experiences," CC stated strongly. "Look at the self-centered greed of executive management! Well, I guess it's believable since the company grew from what was once focused on research and development into a corporation led by finance types."

"A discriminating nightmare," agreed Deborah. "Not because of race, but because it seemed that management was against anyone who was hard-working or trustworthy. A crazy, confusing, de-motivating work environment, that's for sure."

"It was certainly my worst work experience ever," Wendy concurred. "Remember how we counted the days until being transferred out of that unpredictable department. How did we ever survive?"

"Well," CC declared, "praise God that we did!"

Deborah added, "And just look at the great relationships we've maintained over the years. What a wonderful, lovely, good-lookin' group of ladies we are too!"

"You know it!" CC agreed.

"That's us!" Saralyn, Wendy, and Keri joined in.

"Sorry to see this afternoon end," Deborah said, and informed the group, "I've got to get going. I promised that husband of mine that I would try and bring home some dessert. Is there any left?"

As the women busied themselves packing up their gifts and cleaning up some of the mess, Wendy and Keri stated that they had to get going as well. Last-minute goodbyes were exchanged at the front entryway.

"Thank you, CC, for opening up your home for this year's party and for entertaining us," Keri said.

"And, you have been such an excellent, wonderful, kind, elegant hostess. Maybe you wouldn't mind doing it all again next year?" Deborah queried, grinning.

"Hey, wait a minute. I should have seen that one coming. I've had my turn," laughed CC.

Immediately after they had left, Saralyn asked CC, "Are you still coming to church with us tomorrow?"

"You bet. I'm looking forward to it. I think Eddie and April will probably join us."

"Great, the more the merrier."

Chapter Thirteen

Family and friends began to gather just outside the church's main entrance. First Matt and Ben arrived. Next CC, Eddie, and April walked up.

"Hey, Ben, really good to see you here." CC gave his arm a pat.

"Well, Matt here talked me into it. Besides, I wouldn't want to miss hearing Breanne sing."

"Good morning, CC."

"Good morning, Matt."

CC introduced Eddie and April to Matt and Ben. Then Matt nodded toward the church parking lot.

"There's Saralyn now. Looks like Marissa is with her too."

CC explained the presence of Breanne's older sister. "As I understand it, Marissa sometimes comes to church for special occasions. You know, Easter, Mother's Day. Since Breanne is singing in the Christmas program this morning, Saralyn probably talked her into it."

"Good morning, everyone!" Saralyn was visibly pleased to see the group.

"Ben, you came too. I'm so glad you accepted our invitation." Then she said to the rest of the group, "You know, we have been rushing around all morning. Breanne has been here since eight o'clock. I had to drop her off for the eight-thirty service."

Saralyn introduced Marissa. "Everyone, this is Marissa. Marissa, you know Ben and CC. This is Eddie, CC's son, and his friend April."

Marissa politely said hello to everyone.

"And this is Matt."

Matt faced Marissa, as he offered to shake her hand. "Nice to meet you, Marissa. I recognized you from the family pictures on your mother's desk." Then turning toward Saralyn with a smile, he said warmly, "Good morning, Saralyn."

"Good morning, Matt."

Saralyn was extremely glad to see Matt and may not have been entirely successful in hiding that fact. Especially, since her heart started to pound thunderously hard.

As the group entered the church to find seats, CC whispered in her friend's ear. "I saw the way you looked at him. What's going on?"

"Nothing!" Saralyn answered in a quiet but forceful tone. "Like I told you before, we're just friends."

"Right. Mister rugged and good-looking was especially attentive to you. I noticed the way he said his special 'good morning' for your ears only," CC teased.

Before Saralyn had an opportunity to respond, she abruptly stopped walking.

"CC, look over there, that guy sitting down on the other side, toward the back. It's the same man in the gray coat. He's been here maybe once or twice since that first time I saw him a few months ago. He has someone with him today."

They all entered the main, middle aisle of the church and began looking for an empty row of seats.

Ben, who'd overheard Saralyn's earlier remarks about the men in gray coats, commented, "I recognize the younger man. Just can't seem to put my finger on where I've met him before."

As Saralyn guided Marissa into an aisle, she was followed by CC, April, Eddie, Ben, and then Matt.

"Marissa, can you see OK?"

"Yeah, Mom, fine. How long do you think this will last, anyway?"

"I don't know, Marissa. And please, try not to look so miserable, OK, honey? Just enjoy all the great music."

By this time, they had all sat down. Ben whispered something to Matt, but no one else could hear what he'd said. Pastor Dave stood up from his seat at the front of the church and walked up the few steps to the platform where the microphone was.

"Who is that fine-looking man?" CC wanted to know.

"That's the senior pastor of this church, CC," smiled Saralyn.

"Hmm, is he married?"

Saralyn whispered back, "No. Shh. Now, let's listen to what he has to say."

Pastor Dave began to speak. "Good morning, everyone, and welcome. We have a wonderful Christmas program for you. God has blessed this church with many talented individuals. Before we begin our special program, I have a few announcements for you."

He read through the several routine announcements; then at the end he added, "I have been asked to inform you this morning, that effective December 31 of this year, your tithes and offerings will no longer be tax deductible. These changes have recently been made by our government to further ensure separation between church and state. It is my prayer that these changes will not inhibit your giving. The IRS rules are effective beginning January 1, 2000. So please understand that whatever you give before then will be tax deductible. Now, let's all sit back, enjoy, and be blessed by our morning service. First, let us pray."

Pastor Dave asked in prayer that everyone would feel God's presence and be touched by the Christmas program. After he said "amen" and as everyone in the congregation raised their heads, many adults were looking at each other with bewildered expressions on their faces. They were too stunned to say much.

Besides, the program had started.

The children's choir sang first. Ten to twelve kids, ranging in age from four to seven, began singing "Away in a Manger." There were many *oohs* and *aahs* from the audience. You could hear whispers of "They're so darling" and "How cute."

The younger children remained on the stage, and the eight- to eleven-year-old kids joined them. The older children sang "Little Drummer Boy" while one of the smaller boys not-so-gently banged on his drum. There were more soft laughs, *oohs*, and *aahs*, during this performance, in which the four- to seven-year-olds also joined in at the *parum-pum-pum-pums*.

After the junior-high and high-school choir members sang a couple of songs, Breanne's group appeared on stage. Her trio sang "Silent Night," blending their voices beautifully. Saralyn was misty-eyed as she patted Marissa's hand. The friends and family surrounding her were also touched by the performance.

There were then a couple more soloists, during which time the offering was taken. Next, the adult choir came onto the stage for the final several numbers.

As the Christmas service drew toward a close, all of the other performers came back onto the stage, including Pastor Dave, who asked everyone to join together in singing the last song. The congregation stood and sang "Joy to the World." At the end of the song, the performers left the stage and exited the sanctuary first. They were followed by everyone else in the audience.

Saralyn's group gathered outside the church and waited for Breanne. When Breanne finally walked up and joined them, there were many voices at once, praising her performance—so much so that Breanne began to get a little embarrassed.

"Thanks, everyone. During the first service I was nervous, even though we practiced so much. But by the second service we were all more relaxed. Piece of cake."

"Speaking of food, does anyone want to go out for coffee and dessert?" suggested CC. "And why don't we invite Pastor Dave to join us?"

"Good idea," Saralyn agreed. "I was actually thinking the same thing. Maybe, we can ask him what that IRS announcement was all about."

Ben said he couldn't join them and neither could Eddie and April, who had made other plans. Ben went from Matt to Eddie, shaking everyone's hand. He paused and gave Breanne's hand a special pat. "You sounded like an angel."

"Oh, thank you, Ben."

Breanne continued innocently, "Hope to see you back here again sometime soon."

Ben nodded his head and replied, "Well, maybe. We'll see." And as he walked away to the parking lot he said, "See you at work tomorrow, Saralyn. Goodbye, everyone."

Those left standing in front of the church waved goodbyes to Ben, Eddie, and April.

Marissa told Breanne, "Hey, Sis, you sounded pretty good up there."

"Why, thank you," Breanne said, accepting her sister's compliment. "You could be singing too, you know. Your voice is just the same as mine."

"Yeah, Yeah. Come on, I'll drive you home in Mom's car. The rest of them are going out for coffee or something."

After saying their goodbyes to everyone, the two sisters drove home together. This provided them an opportunity to talk without their mom around. Sometimes, when they were getting along with each other, they felt more at ease discussing what was going on in their personal lives if Saralyn was not listening.

Marissa confided in Breanne that she was really beginning to like the mall security guard she'd met. Probably, according to Marissa, more than she'd ever liked anyone before. They'd been able to have long talks whenever they could arrange to take their work breaks together. He was going to school and working at the mall most nights.

So far, they hadn't spent as much time together as they both wanted to. She shared with her younger sister that they were in the process of trying to coordinate the same days off.

Breanne confided in her older sister the fact that a lot of her friends in school had tried out the new lockers. That meant that many more students had the ID chip implanted. Some of the kids had started singling out those students who, so far, avoided getting the chip. Breanne and others like her were definitely being treated as outsiders, and most were not eligible to be in the popular crowd.

So far Breanne had held out without too much of a problem. But now there were beginning to be more and more consequences. She was hurt by being labeled "unpopular" along with the others who resisted following the majority.

The two teenage girls stopped at a video rental store on the way home and decided just to relax and watch a movie for the afternoon. It was not often that they spent time alone together without fighting.

After Saralyn introduced Pastor Dave to CC and Matt, she invited him to meet them at a nearby coffee shop. Pastor Dave accepted her invitation. After they all arrived and had ordered their food, discussion turned to the morning visitors in the gray lab coats.

Pastor Dave let them know that the men had specifically requested that he make the announcement in their presence.

"They asked me to announce the tax changes following the early service and before the Christmas program during the second service."

"I saw them leave while the children were singing," Matt remembered. "Obviously, the timing of the announcements must have been to minimize the amount of time they had to spend in church. Ben whispered to me that he remembered where he had met the younger man."

"Where was that at, Matt?" asked CC.

"Ben met him down at the city's building and planning department when Ben was applying for some permits."

"We haven't done that for more than a year," Saralyn thought back. "Must have been when we needed to put up the back fence. It needed to be nine feet high to block the view of our recycling yard from residential areas. Anyway, I wonder why the WOOS are recruiting people from local city personnel."

Matt filled in some missing pieces. "I have heard that this new world order organization is actively recruiting from local areas. Dave, what does all this mean to you?"

"The WOOS. Is that what people are calling all of these government representatives in the gray coats?"

There were nods and yeses from the other three at the table.

CC explained to Dave that her son Eddie had been seeing the gray coats out at the local military base. Only out there, the representatives were wearing nametags on their coats that said WORLD ORDER ORGANIZATION.

"You know, I really want to search the Scripture for answers. It's the first place to look."

"I feel the same way," CC smiled, and she encouraged him to continue.

Saralyn's eyebrows shot up. She hoped Pastor Dave wasn't uncomfortable with CC's obvious flirting. Actually, it looked like he was enjoying her undisguised personal attention.

Dave continued, "The WOOS did mention that in the near future there might even be some governmental recording of all church services."

Saralyn and CC were shaking their heads in disbelief as they both muttered, "You've got to be kidding."

"Seriously?" Matt added, alarmed. "This is beginning to sound like another country. Around the world, persecution of Christians is tolerated, even encouraged."

"Dear Lord, what next?" wondered CC. "Well, Dave, how long have you been pastor of the Oakbrook Christian Church?"

The foursome chatted for about an hour more over coffee and dessert, enjoying each others' company.

Dave was concerned about what might happen to church attendance and financial support beginning in January. "We need to form prayer-warrior meetings. To me, all of this mysterious activity has a kind of cinematic quality. It's not real yet. I should prepare my words for next week's sermon carefully, just in case the church has already been bugged. My prayer is that we can keep the church doors open as long as possible, regardless of the financial support. God will find a way."

During the afternoon, there was an obvious attraction between Matt and Saralyn. Their eyes met frequently. CC didn't notice her friend's reactions this time around—she was especially interested in what Pastor Dave had to say.

When it neared time to leave, CC asked, "Saralyn, are you still going to pick me up for lunch tomorrow?"

"Sure, I'll do that. We can go to that new place right across the street from your office."

CC and Saralyn walked outside together to the coffee shop's parking lot. Pastor Dave volunteered to drop Saralyn off at her home. Marissa had driven her mom's car home from church, and Dave lived only a half-dozen blocks away from them.

Matt and Saralyn hugged each other goodbye as they had done frequently in the past—usually after one of their long, friendship conversations at the recycling center. This Sunday afternoon was different.

Matt held her a little longer than usual and kept hold of her hand as they slowly walked away from each other, as if he were trying to tell her something.

CC interrupted Saralyn's thoughts as she whispered to her friend, "Maybe there is hope after all. It's possible all the good men in this town are not already married. Perhaps I'll start attending church more regularly with you."

"Hmm, that wouldn't have anything to do with a certain pastor, now, would it? Why don't you just join us for Thursday night Bible study, too!"

"Oh, why thank you for asking. I might just take you up on that. Does he also lead your single's Bible study?"

"Yes, CC, he does. I'll see you tomorrow around 11:45," Saralyn chuckled as she answered quietly. She then climbed into the car where Dave was waiting.

"OK, Saralyn. See you tomorrow."

Later that afternoon, Saralyn wandered into her backyard and over to the rosebushes.

Just look at what beauty God has created, and He allows me to be a caretaker. I didn't think these bushes would ever grow back again after I cut them so far back last winter. But, they've certainly renewed their growth. Some branches are even stronger than before. Soon, it will be time for me to cut them down again.

Then her thoughts turned toward Matt.

These rosebushes are similar to my emotions. Not long ago, my feelings were so numbed I didn't think I was going to feel strongly about anyone ever again. But now, God has renewed my capability and desire to love.

My Savior, my Knight-in-shining-armor is Jesus. He has brought me such peace. He knows best. I just need to let go of my worries, and let Him be the caretaker of my troubles. Am I reading too much into the brief glances from Matt? Does he possibly feel the same way about me as I have begun to feel about him? My prayer is for discernment. CC was right. Love is not the same as some recycled material. God can renew us, and He does.

CHAPTER FOURTEEN

Saralyn picked up the telephone late Monday morning to give CC a call. She needed to let her know that she was running behind. There had been an unexpected invoice problem that needed sorting out first. She dialed her friend's work number and reached the voice message system for the Children's Welfare and Adoption Agency (CWAA).

After following the recorded voice prompts, she left a message: "Good morning, CC. It's me. Hey, listen, I'm running just about ten minutes late, but I'm leaving now. Hope you're not standing outside in front of the building right now, waiting. See you in a few minutes."

It normally took about ten to twelve minutes, depending on traffic, for Saralyn to drive to the building where CC's agency was located. When she arrived there, Saralyn took the elevator to reach CC's third floor office, but she discovered that it was empty.

As Saralyn looked around CC's office, she saw that there were a few new pictures scattered around. Some were on cork boards, others in frames. Some were of the children for whom the agency had found homes.

"That's the most satisfying part of the job," CC had once confided to Saralyn. The application process for adoption, or to become foster care parents, can be burdensome and long. When a match was made with a couple who had been thoroughly screened, that was a very rewarding experience, even when the placements were only temporary for some children.

About five minutes passed with no sign of CC. *Oh well,* Saralyn sighed to herself, *I'll just sit and wait a few minutes for her to get back from wherever she is. If CC doesn't make it back in soon, I'll check the ladies restroom.*

Just then, CC walked in. She looked distraught. "You are not going to believe the memo I received earlier this morning!"

"What is it, CC?"

"Here, read it." In a rushed manner, she handed Saralyn a one-page memo on agency letterhead. "I've been checking around all morning to try and figure out just who knows what."

Saralyn read through the memo:

Children's Welfare and Adoption Agency
CWAA

MEMORANDUM
To All Personnel:

Beginning immediately, all Agency employees will have the opportunity to participate in the new ID program. It is currently an elective program that will ensure those who participate instant access to all computer files. In addition, for those who volunteer, it will eliminate the need to use your security badges for access into your respective buildings.

The Board of Directors and I hope that all Agency employees will take advantage of this new technology. It requires that a very small identity chip be implanted into the top of your hand. We have begun implanting these chips into children who have become wards of the state during the past thirty days. The nurses have been trained to do this simple procedure during routine physicals, and there have been no ill effects whatsoever.

As always, we encourage all personnel to take advantage of the suggestion boxes centrally located in all of the departments. Please provide us with any comments for management that you may have.

Season's Greetings to All.

"I've been concerned about the shortcuts being taken in finding qualified adoptive and foster care parents, because of the increases in abandoned babies. But now this. I never knew this was going on." CC was visibly upset and shaken. "How could I not see this?"

"According to the memo, it's only been going on for thirty days. Don't be so hard on yourself," Saralyn soothed.

"It just breaks my heart. This is where it starts, you know." CC choked back tears of frustration. "So subtle. The WOOS start with the most innocent who have no voice, and I can't do anything about it. This is all so frustrating. Did you catch the part about the ID chip being currently an elective program for agency employees?"

Saralyn remembered exactly what the memo said, and she was well aware of the similarities to what her daughter was experiencing. "Just like Breanne's high school!"

CC asked Saralyn, "Do you want to come and see a couple of the new babies at the clinic before we go?"

"Yes. Can we do that? You know I'd really love to."

As they walked down the hall, CC explained to Saralyn that there were serious problems in addition to the increase in abandoned children. Many of the babies were exhibiting unusual behavior. The mothers may have been addicted to different combinations of MADS.

When they entered the large room where most of the children were, Saralyn looked around. The furnishings were out of the ordinary. Except, of course, for the usual cribs and changing tables. Attempts had been made to decorate the walls with a few colorful posters. One poster was of a Disney movie; another depicted popular cartoon characters. There were large quantities of toys lying around. Mainly what Saralyn noticed, were the sad, vacant, drugged faces of most the babies and children.

One baby girl, whom Saralyn bent to pick up, was approximately three months old. She had been at the clinic for about two and a half months. The baby they were told, was jaundiced since shortly after coming to the clinic, and she still appeared to be a little yellow.

"You know, my grandmother used to say that back in her day when a baby's coloring didn't look right, the mothers would place the cradle in the sunniest window of the house," Saralyn recalled. "Or they would somehow place the baby up on a windowsill to catch as much sun as possible."

The baby's eyes were only half opened, and she was not alert. "She seems pretty lethargic." Saralyn handed the little girl to CC and picked up one of the newborn baby boys. "He's so small."

The nurse on duty was wearing a crisply starched, white uniform. She informed them that he weighed only four and a half pounds at birth, full term. He was gaining weight slowly and was progressing as well as they could expect.

This little boy had such big, alert, trusting, brown eyes, and lots of dark hair. So tiny and helpless, small, and completely dependent. Saralyn thought, *These babies, and all children, deserve to have healthy parents.*

At that time, the nurse decided it would be no problem if she left the daycare center for just a moment. She felt comfortable doing so, since CC was there now and had relieved her in the past for short coffee breaks and such. She had been wanting to use the restroom for almost an hour.

"I'll be back in just a minute."

"No problem," CC reassured her. "We can manage to watch this small group for a few minutes. Just take your time, Allison."

After the nurse walked out, CC put down the baby girl she had been holding and reached for the hand of the little boy that Saralyn still held in her arms.

She whispered to Saralyn, "Look at this little guy's left hand."

There between his thumb and forefinger was an adhesive bandage strip.

"Let's take a look under the Band-Aid." She quickly lifted the end of it, and sure enough, there were several tiny stitches underneath.

"Wish I could rip this ID chip right out of him."

"I know, CC. Let's try to remain calm."

As the nurse walked back in, CC and Saralyn were cooing over the baby boy. "Does he have a name yet?"

"No, I don't think so, just a number," Allison answered.

"Oh well, maybe we could give him a nickname, just temporarily."

"Actually, from now on, we've all been advised not to do that, you know," the nurse replied uncomfortably. "It's easier on everyone not to develop any attachments."

"Hmm, OK." CC turned to Saralyn, "Well, we'd better get going." She then nodded toward the nurse, "Good seeing you again, Allison."

As the friends headed back to CC's office, Saralyn asked with concern, "What are you going to do, CC?"

"I don't know. I'm thinking of leaving this job."

"Don't do that, CC. Let's go for lunch and we'll talk more."

"I'm not even hungry anymore."

"I'm not either, really. We'll eat light and quick."

They stopped briefly by CC's office to pick up her purse. Then they walked across the street to a corner minimall where a new deli was located. Before they left the building, however, Saralyn could have sworn she caught a glimpse of Marcy. It was just a side view from down the hall, and she had met Daniel's sister only twice. But it did look like her. Saralyn mentioned it to CC just as they were walking through the restaurant door.

"Maybe, you can check on Marcy's status later. I'll bet she does work in your building, CC. She was yet another person wearing a gray lab coat."

We're surrounded! Marcy could even be one of the doctors implanting those ID chips, Saralyn thought to herself. "OK, CC, let's get a booth if there's one available." Once they settled in, Saralyn consoled her friend and asked her not to give up. "Those children need you."

CC, with her eyes gazing out the deli window, realized that Saralyn was right. "I know, but it's just that the government has gained more and more control. I can't make any decisions of significance anymore without their approval. Now all those children that come through here and become wards of the state will also have these chips implanted in them. ID chips, Saralyn! Without a voice of their own to say no." CC sighed heavily and continued, "You know, a few weeks ago, I remember commenting to one of the nurses about Band-Aids on a couple of babies' hands. She said they started withdrawing blood with butterfly needles from the top of the hand, because it was easier on smaller children and babies. That made sense to me at the time."

The soups they ordered arrived, and they both took a few bites now and then between sentences. By the end of their quick meal, CC had calmed down quite a bit.

"I wonder how many others know about all this and approve of what's going on. You're right, Saralyn! I do need to stay here. No one else really talks to these children, except for a few of the volunteer senior citizens who visit once or twice a week."

As Saralyn actively listened, nodding her head in agreement, CC made plans.

"Maybe I can find out more about the WOOS. Maybe I'll give your Pastor Dave a call." Thinking of him cheered her up just a little. CC questioned Saralyn about Dave. "Do you know how long he has been a single parent? What about his kids? When and where did he go to seminary?"

Saralyn grinned at her friend's curiosity. It was the first time either of them had smiled all day.

"Come on. We'd better get going. I'll walk you to your car," CC volunteered.

"Have you decided to join Bible study on Thursday night?" Saralyn asked.

"I'm thinking about it. You know, I'll probably see you there."

"OK, CC. Take a deep breath and pray. I want to tell you something." Saralyn knew how important it was to be supportive of each other. "Your friendship is very valuable to me. If there is anything I can do, call me—anytime. Sounds a little corny, but just like the song, I'll be there. Remember what you like to quote."

"What's that?"

"If God is for us, who can be against us?"

"You're right about that. I'm going to put on my battle armor with reinforcements this time and head back to work. Drive carefully, Saralyn."

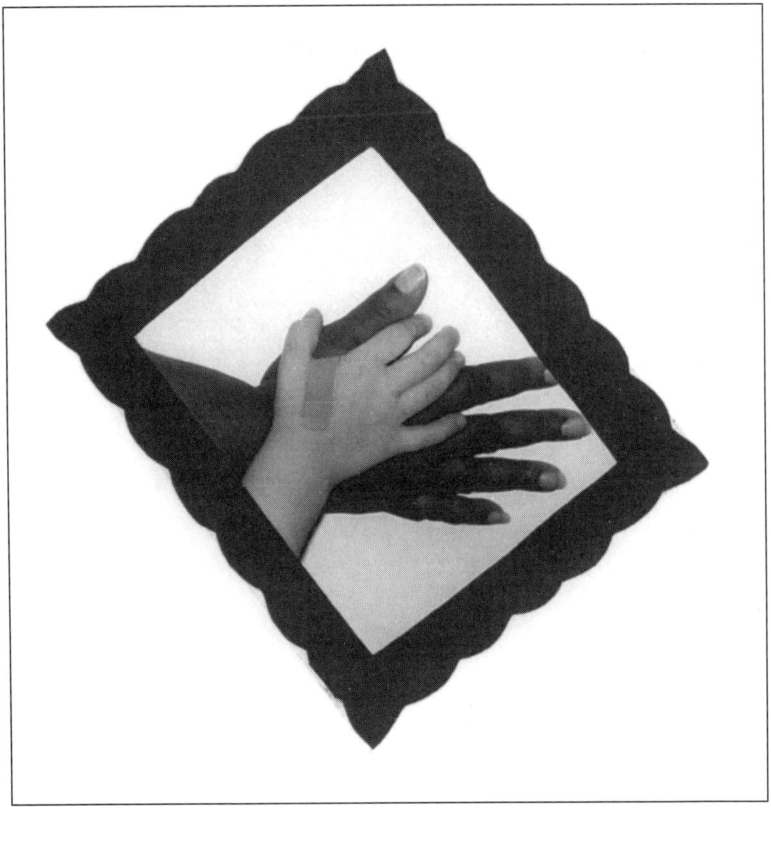

Chapter Fifteen

Saralyn went back to work that Monday afternoon, but she had a difficult time really concentrating. Today, she especially looked forward to sharing these troubling events with Matt after work.

"CC was visibly upset, Matt. You can just imagine. At first she wanted to quit, but I think she'll stay. You know, she's one of the few at that agency who seems to truly care about what happens to those children."

"How long do you think this has really been going on?" Matt was interested.

"Well, the memo did say thirty days, but you're right to question the timing. One never knows for sure."

"Now that these identity implants are pretty much out in the open, the WOOS will just wait for the public to become tolerant of the whole idea."

"I think you're right," Saralyn agreed.

Matt suggested that they walk outside to enjoy the mild December weather.

As he opened the door for Saralyn to exit, she grazed him gently in passing. Then as she sat down on the bench and he moved to sit next to her, Saralyn bumped Matt's arm. These brief touches were electric.

The smell of Matt was intoxicating. Not that he was wearing any overpowering cologne. It was more subtle, natural, definitely all male. There was no flirting, no sexual innuendoes. Just his nearness caused her to breathe irregularly!

What if he is interested in me as a friend only, and a sister Christian. Does he feel this intensity? I hope he can't hear my heart pounding.

Saralyn attempted to refocus her thoughts on the visit with CC and the children at the agency. While she retold more of the days events at CC's workplace, Matt listened attentively, and then he commented.

"I think it's a good idea for CC to stay at the agency. I believe the wisest move would be to not make much of a fuss—at least not now. I'm sure the WOOS are expecting some disagreement, but she needs to keep complaints or protests to a minimum and under control. It is certainly best for now that there be quiet resistance, in order to do the most good and be the most effective in the long run."

Saralyn was crying softly now. The tears were from fatigue and frustration more than anything. She tried unsuccessfully to hide them from Matt. He reached up, placed both his hands on her shoulders, and held her firmly.

"Listen, Saralyn. We know what's happening here. Remember that Satan, the true enemy, is at work here on earth. He's sneaky and strong, but we know who is by far much stronger. God is omnipotent."

"I know, Matt. Thank you for listening. I guess I'm just a little tired emotionally. It's been quite a month."

Matt's grip on her shoulders turned softer as he pulled her in toward him. He gathered her in his arms as they sat on the bench in the midst of the rosebushes. It seemed the most natural thing for Saralyn to lean into him, as if they were meant to be molded together. She felt his warmth, his strength, all at once. Matt's hand stroked her hair gently. His face was so close to hers.

As Matt's breath neared her face, he held her chin in his right hand and brought her lips to his. He kissed her thoroughly, their lips parting after several seconds. She felt the breathless sensation throughout her entire body, right down to her toes. When his lips left hers, Saralyn opened her eyes. He held her gaze, looking deeply into her eyes. The blood was pounding through her veins.

Matt's arms were still around her when he said huskily, "Your lips are as soft as I imagined them to be." And then he added, "I've been wanting to do that for a long time now."

Saralyn steadied herself by taking a deep breath and then responded with a smile, "I'm glad you finally did."

After several moments of quiet, they began to discuss the recent events further. As Saralyn laid her cheek against Matt's chest, she could feel the vibrations of his voice rumbling beneath her.

It was decided between the two of them that Breanne would be in no immediate trouble by not volunteering right away for the lockers at school. The implanted chips were not mandatory yet for those who had a voice. At CC's workplace, as well, only the youngest were currently involuntary victims.

What might be more complicated was convincing others, such as family, friends, and loved ones, not to take and get hooked on the mood-altering drugs. Many people were becoming too complacent, unaccountable, and easily influenced, when they got hooked on MADS. If they ran out or tried to quit cold turkey, they became irrational and unreasonable. It was obviously best not to start at all. However, if they did and wanted to stop, they would have to go through a slow and difficult withdrawal.

Matt and Saralyn realized it was getting late and that they should finish locking up the recycling center. It wasn't easy to make that first move away from their new found closeness.

"CC was going to give Pastor Dave a call and keep him updated," Saralyn informed Matt. "Besides, did you notice she has a bit of a crush on him already."

"Dave did mention something to me about that. While you two were in the restroom at the coffee shop yesterday, he said he thought CC might be interested in him. Actually, what he said was that he hoped he read her signals right, because he's interested in and would like to get to know her better too."

"Oh, really. I wonder if I should tell her just yet. It would certainly cheer her up."

"Would you be available to get together later this evening, Saralyn, and talk? There are some more things I'd like to discuss."

"Yes, sure. I'd like that. How about after dinner, around seven-thirty or seven-forty-five?"

It was difficult for Matt and Saralyn to let go of each other. Once they had sampled a small taste of affection after being without it for so long—years—it was very hard to move away from it. However, they finally untangled themselves, stood up, and made plans to meet later that evening at Saralyn's place.

At home, Marissa was distraught. The security guard she had been hanging out with missed his last two nights of work. He didn't answer his phone either. His family was Hispanic, his parents illegal aliens. The guard, however, had been born in the United States.

Marissa did not know what could have happened. Rumors were going around the mall that his whole family was deported. Many Hispanic families were missing.

Marissa also told her mom about the owner of the shop where she worked. Suddenly and unexpectedly, there was a new owner. No one was talking about what might have happened to her old boss. She had heard that all of the Oakbrook Mall store owners needed to cooperate with the WOOS. Maybe the Lotions 'n' Lipsticks manager hadn't in some way.

Saralyn comforted her daughter and decided to take the opportunity to suggest that she now come to work for her at the recycling center. "Marissa, you have always been good with numbers, just like Andrew. The invoices and paperwork have been piling up, and you can work at least thirty hours a week."

Saralyn offered Marissa a small raise from what she was earning at the mall. Andrew had stopped showing up altogether for his part-time accounting job at the recycling center, and this new arrangement might be a solution for more than one problem. At least for now.

Later that evening, while Breanne, Marissa, Saralyn, and Matt were watching TV, another mystery unfolded. They realized that another news station was not on at its normal time and channel.

Matt explained that he tried watching CNN earlier in the day, but it had been temporarily off the air. All he could find while channel surfing were sitcom reruns and some raunchy talk show. The only news channel available to them tonight was one that sounded as if it were censored and under government control.

At approximately eight o'clock, there was a telephone call from CC. Matt, Marissa, and Breanne could hear only one side of the conversation. They heard Saralyn utter in a shocked voice, "Oh no, CC! How did it happen? Why? So much is happening so fast." There was disbelief in her voice. "I just can't believe it. Yes, I'll call Wendy. Call me tomorrow when you find out more, OK? Or I'll call you. Goodnight, CC."

As Saralyn slowly put the receiver down, she turned toward the concerned group.

"What's wrong, Mom? What happened?" Both daughters were now standing at her side.

"Keri is dead." Saralyn tried to take a deep breath. While swallowing with difficulty, she attempted to relay what details were known so far. "It looks like suicide. She apparently overdosed on something. CC said that she had been calling Keri for a couple of days, and when she finally reached her, she could tell something was wrong. CC asked and Keri admitted how much she needed the medications to relax." Saralyn was struggling, to maintain her composure. "I blame these new MADS. So many doctors have been prescribing them."

Saralyn faced Matt and tried to explain, "Keri was one of the gals I used to work with. We all go to lunch occasionally. I just can't believe she's gone."

The tears were visible now, making their trails slowly down Saralyn's cheeks. Marissa and Breanne sympathized with their mom—in part because they were not used to seeing Saralyn upset, but also because, over the years, both girls had met and gotten to know Keri a little. They also began to cry.

"So many sad and strange things are happening," Marissa blurted.

"Let's turn off the TV for now and talk about this," Matt suggested. "I'm sincerely sorry about your friend, Saralyn."

Matt gave her a comforting hug, and then the four of them sat down in the living room.

Saralyn, continued to cry quietly throughout the rest of the evening.

"I think more pieces of the puzzle are beginning to fall into place," Matt theorized. "It is possible that the government believes they will be more successful influencing the adult population that get hooked on MADS, while implementing the implanting of ID chips. As long as they easily prescribe or approve reimbursement for these drugs, people will become addicted to them."

"I can't help thinking that maybe, just maybe, there was something more I could have done. I should have followed up on promised phone calls," Saralyn lamented, shaking her head in disbelief.

Matt suggested sympathetically, "It's reasonable to expect that most everyone who knew Keri will feel some guilt in one way or another. I've read that many individuals who have committed suicide, or who have attempted it, don't really want to die. It's just that they don't have the strength to live another day. They feel as if nobody loves them. They feel unwanted. We are the lucky ones, you know—all of us who realize that God loves us, always, every day. God's love can definitely provide feelings of security and peace when crazy things are happening all around you." Then Matt offered to tell the group a story from the Bible.

Saralyn had mentioned earlier that she wanted to tell her daughters the New Testament parable of the ten virgins. Now because she was too upset to recount it, Matt volunteered.

Saralyn sat on the living room couch, sandwiched closely in between Marissa and Breanne. Matt was sitting on a smaller, matching loveseat directly across from them. He leaned forward and began to tell them the story.

"This is a parable that Jesus tells us. It's recorded in Matthew, which is the first Gospel of the New Testament, and the book of the Bible my parents named me after.

In Jesus' words:

> The Kingdom of Heaven is like the ten virgins who took their lamps and went out to meet the bridegroom. Now five of them were wise, and five were foolish. Those who were foolish took their lamps and took no oil with them, but the wise took oil in their vessels with their lamps. But while the bridegroom was delayed, they all slumbered and slept.
> And at midnight a cry was heard: "Behold, the bridegroom is coming; go out to meet him!"
> Then all those virgins arose and trimmed their lamps. And the foolish said to the wise, "Give us some of your oil, for our lamps are going out."
> But the wise answered, saying, "No, lest there should not be enough for us and you; but go rather to those who sell, and buy for yourselves."
> And while they went to buy, the bridegroom came, and those who were ready went in with him to the wedding; and the door was shut.
> Afterward the other virgins came also, saying, "Lord, Lord, open to us!"
> But he answered and said, "Assuredly I say to you, I do not know you."
> Watch therefore, for you know neither the day nor the hour in which the Son of Man is coming."

Saralyn explained further: "I know you both have heard this story before, since you've grown up going to church. It's important to understand the meaning. The door being shut to the virgins is like being shut out of the kingdom of heaven. The unwise virgins were not ready. We don't know when Christ will return, but we must be prepared. The parable of the ten virgins explains the need for making our decision to believe now, not later."

Saralyn was noticeably shaken by the death of her friend. But she managed to instruct her daughters, "We must believe!" Then, with a heavy heart, she suggested, "Well, listen guys. Why don't you think about getting ready for bed."

Marissa and Breanne headed toward their bedrooms. They both said goodnight to Matt, and gave their mom a hug.

After they had gone into their rooms, Saralyn was grateful and complimentary, "Thank you, Matt. You tell a good story."

"Well, you know, Jesus was the storyteller. Saralyn, why don't you come over here and sit with me for a few minutes."

"In just a second. Let me give Wendy a call first." Saralyn dialed the number, and Wendy answered quickly, as if she were standing right next to the phone.

"Wendy, this is Saralyn."

"Oh, Saralyn, did you hear about Keri?"

"Yes, CC called to tell me. That's why I'm calling."

Wendy was upset. She shared her most recent memories of the last time they were all together. "I can't believe it. Keri! We just had our Christmas brunch. She seemed fine, didn't she?"

"Well, actually Wendy, Keri had been struggling," Saralyn offered gently. "Now, I'm really worried about her kids too. What's going to happen to them?"

"They'll probably go to live with George. What a tragedy."

"I know, Wendy. This is awful."

They were both crying softly as they agreed to talk again tomorrow. Saralyn hung up the phone, walked over to the loveseat, and sat down next to Matt.

He put his arm lightly around her shoulders.

"You know, Matt. I worked for years with people who profess to be Christians. There was certainly no way you would have ever guessed it by their actions! Many women at work who said they went to church on Sunday would stab you in the back on Monday. I want to be a positive example of Christianity. I should have called Keri more often. Maybe I could have invited her to church with us. For that matter, I should have spoken more of being a Christian to Jessica. You know, she's the other woman I used to work with. I told you about running in to her shopping at the Oakbrook Mall the other day. Tomorrow, I'm going to make it a point to invite Wendy to church," Saralyn added assertively.

Matt gave her shoulders a gentle squeeze. Then he said, "A lot of unusual things have happened, and it seems as if they're happening fast. My timing may not be terrific here, but who knows when a better time will be. What I'm trying to say is, Saralyn, I hope we can start spending more time together." He added, less nervously, "I want to be with you more often."

Saralyn could not remember having felt so many different emotions all within such a short period of time. There was overwhelming sadness, confusion, and grief over the death of a friend. There was elation along with relief over the fact that the man she had fallen in love with seemed to be experiencing similar feelings for her.

A renewed love.

Matt asked her more directly now, "Do you think we can spend a lot more time together?"

She managed to whisper while nodding yes, "I think that can be arranged."

Matt comfortably draped his arm around Saralyn and pulled her closer to him. She felt warm and safe in his arms. How wonderful it would be to spend countless hours exactly like this, wrapped in warmth and love—just like the quilt that she had tried to imagine. There was hope in comfort.

Matt was planning ahead. "We move forward from here, Saralyn. We can be an encouragement to each other. You and I can pray together, worship, and share Christ with others together, even if it ends up being only a few of us at a time, as Dave fears, or our worship goes underground."

Saralyn could once again feel his breath near her face. She welcomed the vibrations of his voice under her cheek, as she rested against the side of his chest.

"Never forget, this is a war between the enemy and God. The enemy is not you or me. Although we can be our own worst enemy at times, Satan is the true enemy!" Matt excitedly continued, "Never forget, Saralyn. We first must claim courage from God's promises and His amazing grace before marching into battle. They are found in the Bible and through prayer. We were created to spread the good news of salvation. We can do so in many ways. One way is by example—by our lives and how we live them. In that way we can show others the peace that is possible when dealing with all the mysteries around Oakbrook and throughout the world. As Christians, we should always remember that we are fighting on the winning team!"

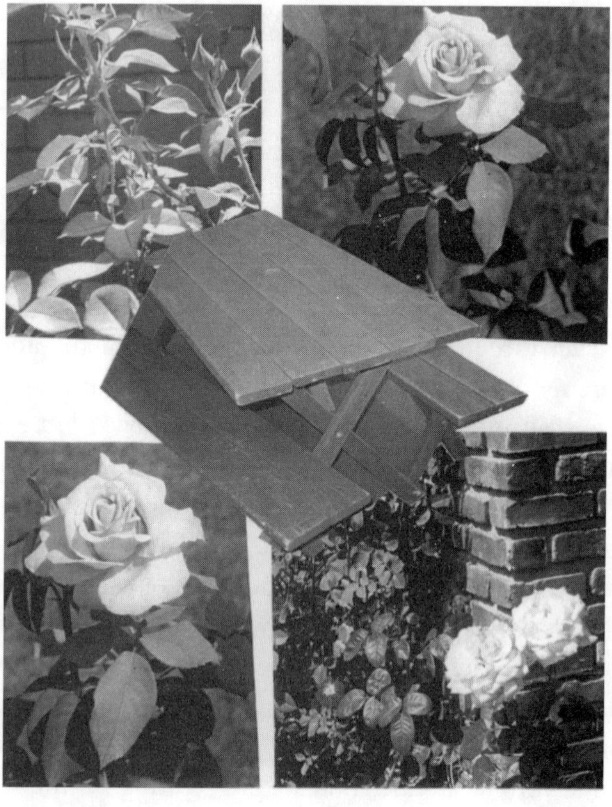

To order additional copies of

Love Renewed in Oakbrook City

send $7.95 plus $4.95 shipping and handling to

Books, Etc.
P.O. Box 1406
Mukilteo, WA 98275

or have your credit card ready and call

(800) 917-BOOK (2665)